AN ENIGMATIC DISAPPEARANCE

ALSO BY RODERIC JEFFRIES

A Maze of Murders
An Artistic Way to Go
An Arcadian Death
Death Takes Time
Murder Confounded
Murder's Long Memory
A Fatal Fleece
Too Clever by Half
Dead Clever
Death Trick
Relatively Dangerous
Almost Murder
Layers of Deceit
Three and One Make Five
Deadly Petard
Unseemly End
Just Deserts
Murder Begets Murder
Troubled Deaths
Two-Faced Death
Mistakenly in Mallorca
Dead Man's Bluff
A Traitor's Crime
A Deadly Marriage
Death in the Coverts
Dead Against the Lawyers
An Embarrassing Death
The Benefits of Death
Exhibit No. Thirteen
Evidence of the Accused

AN ENIGMATIC DISAPPEARANCE

Roderic Jeffries

St. Martin's Minotaur
New York

www.minotaurbooks.com

ISBN 0-312-26583-2

First published in Great Britain by Collins Crime,
an imprint of HarperCollins*Publishers*

First U.S. Edition: October 2000

10 9 8 7 6 5 4 3 2 1

AN ENIGMATIC DISAPPEARANCE

CHAPTER 1

January was a month of many moods. An icy wind from the north accompanied the New Year. On the seventh, the wind was from the south and it was warm and laden with a very fine sand that dusted everything; on the seventeenth, there was snow on the mountains down to the two-hundred-metre level; on the thirty-first, the sky was cloudless, the temperature was over twenty, and those birds which had escaped being illegally shot were singing as if spring had arrived.

Cora returned to the pool patio. 'That was Ada on the phone.' She sat. In appearance as well as character, she provided a sharp contrast to her husband. She possessed the undefined features of someone easily forgotten and if challenged, even on a matter of no importance, became diffident.

'What did the barmaid want?' Keane asked.

'I do wish you wouldn't call her that,' Cora said plaintively. 'She's not really so awful.'

'That depends on the degree of one's magnanimity.'

'But look how she gave the animal refuge enough money for the new kennels they so needed to be built. She does a lot of good on the quiet.'

'So quietly that we invariably all hear about it.'

'That's being uncharitable.'

'Realistic. And if she funded another dozen kennels, she'd still remain a barmaid by design as well as habit.'

For once, she ventured a shaft of humorous criticism. 'I thought men favoured barmaids?'

'Only when young. Cheap goods wear out quickly.'

'I . . . I do wish you wouldn't say things like that – it makes people think.'

'I doubt a host of angels could work that miracle . . . You've still not told me what Ada wanted.'

'She's invited us to a party on Wednesday week.'

'So you remembered a prior invitation?'

'Well, no . . . I mean . . .'

'You're not telling me you accepted?'

'But you always say how nice it is to drink real champagne and not cava and to eat a canapé that's more smoked salmon than bread.'

'Insufficient compensation in her case.'

'Marjory was talking about her yesterday and said she is rough, but she doesn't try to hide behind a screen of social lies.'

'She must have heard someone say that – she could never think it up on her own.'

'Marjory's not really as stupid as you think.'

'Perhaps she couldn't be.'

There was a brief silence, broken by Cora. 'You will go to Ada's, won't you?'

'You've left me with little option other than a grumbling appendix.'

'I'm sure you'll really enjoy it.'

'My dear, you have a remarkable capacity for self-deception.'

There was a streak of stubbornness in her which sometimes surfaced – often when it would have been more politic to keep it hidden. 'Maybe she can be a bit of a mouthful, but at least she's not like so many people and doesn't try to make out she's what she isn't.'

'You are no doubt referring very indirectly to Rino?'

'She's never tried to call him her nephew, has she, or make out they're just good friends?'

'That merely proves that in order to lead a civilized life, one must be a hypocrite.' He stood. 'Another drink?'

'No, thanks.'

He went indoors. She closed her eyes, enjoying the warmth of the sun, and thought about their daughter in England. Pam's last letter had seemed to hint that something was wrong. Undergraduate life could lead to such awful trouble . . .

Keane returned to the patio, glass in hand. As he sat, he said: 'You look like Atlas on a rough day.'

'How d'you mean?'

'The world on your shoulders is weighing even more than usual.'

'Oh! . . . I was thinking about Pam.'

'What disaster are you allotting her today?'

'Her letter is worrying.'

'I told you, there's nothing in it to ring any alarm bells.'

'I do hope you're right.'

'I make a habit of being so.' He drank. 'According to the BBC news, England's all but disappearing under the rain. The news certainly increases the pleasure of the sun here.'

It occurred to her that he often seemed to gain pleasure from other's misfortunes – she hastily dismissed the thought and chided herself for disloyalty.

He looked at his watch. 'We must be off in ten minutes.'

'Off where?'

'We're due at Winnie and Vernon's at half past.'

'What are you talking about?'

'Lunch.'

'You're saying we've been invited there?'

'It would be a grave social solecism to arrive at lunchtime without an invitation. Not, of course, that Vernon would appreciate the fact.'

'You never told me.'

'Of course I did. It's your wandering memory at fault again.'

She didn't argue, even though certain he had never mentioned the invitation. She tried to work out how best to deal with the meal that was cooking.

The Picketts lived in an urbanizacíon which stretched partway up a hill that was almost a mountain. Because of the steepness of the land on which their house was built, it had four floors, from each of which there was a dramatic view across to the bay. It suffered one disadvantage. In heavy rainstorms, which occurred more frequently than tourist information suggested, a waterfall poured across the road, down the steep, curving drive, and into the house from which its only escape was through the sitting-room and out across the patio.

Winnie cut into her steak. 'It's quite tender!' There was

9

a note of surprise in her voice. 'Maybe for once I needn't apologize. D'you know, the other day I asked one of the butchers why they didn't hang the meat longer and he couldn't understand what I was talking about. I'm sure they sell the meat in the shops as soon as the animal's dead.'

'At least,' Keane said, 'we must give them credit for waiting that long. Other primitive tribes slice a chunk off a living animal so that in a few weeks' time they'll be able to do the same thing again.'

'You really do say the most disgusting things! I can't think how Cora puts up with you.'

'By being very conscious of the privilege of doing so.' He spoke across the table to Cora. 'Is that so, my sweet?'

She smiled uncertainly.

Winnie said: 'We had lunch at the Ogdens' the other day and Sabrina must have gone to a lot of trouble to make the steak-and-kidney pie, but the meat really was just like leather.'

'Cooking's never been Sabrina's speciality,' Pickett said.

'Could we for once keep the conversation clean?'

He ignored his wife. 'I suppose you two have heard the latest whispers about Sabrina?'

'And people say it's women who gossip!'

He tapped the side of his nose. 'There's more than one fortune been made on the back of gossip . . . They say she's become very friendly with someone. I'll give you ten to one you can't guess who that someone is.'

'With so many runners, I'd want much better odds,' Keane said.

Pickett reached across the table to pick up the bottle of wine, refilled his glass. 'Rino.'

'Well, well!' Keane teased a crumb of bread on his sideplate. 'Usually a barmaid gives short change, not suffers it.'

CHAPTER 2

Sabrina drew into the catered parking bay, switched off the engine, opened the driving door of the BMW and stepped out into the fierce July sun. She turned back to pick up her handbag and a plastic shopping bag and to shut and lock the doors, made her way between the rows of cars to the clinic. The nearer she approached the large building, the more mentally cold she felt. She hated hospitals. When she'd been small, she had had to spend weeks in one and the memory of her bewildered fear had never left her. Bevis had wanted her to stay with him in the hospital, as was customary; she'd explained why she couldn't, but he hadn't understood.

A man held the right-hand swing door open for her and she smiled her thanks at this unusual courtesy. Her smile brought brief, eager hope. As she went inside, she wondered if every single Spaniard between fifteen and seventy saw himself as Don Juan?

The reception area was crowded and very noisy, thanks to the many uncontrolled children. Among the expatriates, it was assumed that every local was born half deaf since nothing else could explain the tolerance of unnecessary noise. The doors of a lift were open and she stepped inside to find only one couple there. The man asked her something which she guessed to be what floor she wanted, his open admiration earning an angry look from his companion. She said, 'Three', mispronouncing even that single word.

On the third floor, she walked along the corridor, her pace becoming ever slower as she neared room 315. She came to a halt, squared her shoulders, opened the door and called out: 'It's me!' Her voice was bright and betrayed none of her emotions.

There was a short passage, to the left of which was the

bathroom, and then the room came into view. Ogden was sitting in bed, propped up by pillows. She put handbag and shopping bag down on the settee, crossed to the bed and kissed him. She was grateful that he smelled slightly sweeter than he had the other day.

'Why didn't you come yesterday?' was his bad-tempered greeting, as she straightened up.

'I had one of my terrible headaches and simply couldn't, much as I longed to.'

'Why didn't you phone me, then?'

'I just wasn't up to doing even that.'

'I phoned you at home to find out what was going on and there wasn't any answer.'

'Did you? And you thought the worst had happened and I'd fallen off a ladder and broken my neck? You poor love! I took three of those pills which stop the worst of the pain and they knocked me right out. I must have slept through the ringing.'

'Why d'you keep getting these heads?'

'I wish I knew. When we've got you better, I must see someone. I suppose it could just be I need glasses. I so don't want to have to wear them . . . But that's more than enough about me. Much more important, how are you? You look brighter.'

'I don't feel it.'

He was showing his age; all sixty-eight years of it. His complexion was grey, his cheeks were sunken, the lines in his face had deepened, and stubble added an air of old-man slovenliness. 'Poor darling, what a nightmare it's been. It was so nearly . . .' She was unable to finish.

'Perhaps it would have been better if I had died.'

'Don't say such a ghastly thing,' she said, pandering to his desire for excessive sympathy. 'If you knew how I prayed and prayed for you . . .'

'A waste of time.'

'Something worked the miracle. I've brought you something to help cheer you up.' She went over to the settee to pick up the shopping bag, handed this to him. He brought out a bottle of red wine and another of whisky.

He dropped them at his side, leaned back, closed his eyes, and groaned.

'Shall I pour you a whisky?'

'No.'

'Then how about some wine? It's the special Lan you like. And people keep saying how good it is to drink red wine; makes one live longer.'

'The sooner I die, the better.'

'You mustn't go on and on saying things like that.'

'If you felt as I do, you'd understand.'

She leaned over to place her cheek against his. 'Poor, poor bunnikins. But when you're better, which I know will be soon, we'll enjoy ourselves so much you'll want to live for ever.' She left the bedside and went over to the settee to sit. 'What did the doctor say this morning?'

'How would I know? Why are they so stupid that the doctors don't speak English? I told him, my cheeks still hurt, my throat's agony, and my stomach feels as if it's being minced up. All he could do was gabble away in Spanish, not caring whether or not I understood.'

'Couldn't you catch anything he said?'

'No. You know what's really going on, don't you?'

'What?'

'He doesn't give a damn how I am because all the time he's laughing at me.'

'That's impossible. Doctors never laugh at their patients.'

'Maybe they don't in England. Here, everything's different.' He stared through the window, looking at, but not seeing, the distant range of mountains that were topped by an intensely blue sky in which one small orphan cloud was drifting towards the east. 'I took every possible care. I made certain it was always less than a gram. You told me the wrong amount.'

'No, I didn't.'

'Then how did it happen?'

'D'you think that perhaps . . .' She stopped.

'What?'

'Well, maybe you could have mixed up the weights because you'd had a little too much to drink . . .'

'Of course I couldn't, even if they do have such a bloody silly system of weights.' He chewed his lower lip for a few seconds. 'The bastard was laughing at me! He won't find it funny when he's my age.'

He was, she thought, suffering as much from a sense of humiliation as from physical pain. A few weeks before their marriage, she'd been having lunch with Nina, who had been her best friend from time to time. 'He's a pompous old fart,' Nina had said in her husky voice which had so captivated a visiting American colonel, 'but that'll mean he'll never see what's going on under his nose so you'll be free to do your own thing. A recipe for the perfect marriage.'

'What are you thinking?' he asked.

'I was remembering how I was with Nina one day and she collapsed and had to be rushed to hospital. To begin with, the doctors were very grim-faced, but then she surprised them by taking a sudden turn for the better. I was so relieved when I heard what had happened, but it was as nothing to when the doctor told me you'd live. That was like . . . like being reborn.'

'I couldn't stand Nina.'

'I know. It was such a pity because she could be very amusing.'

'At other people's expense.'

'She could be a bit naughty with the things she said. But she could also be very complimentary. She knew you didn't like her and that made her sad, but she still said what a nice man you were and how she was sure we'd have a great time together.'

'She said that?'

'Yes.'

'You surprise me.'

'Quite recently I read that the perfect wife tries to give her husband a little surprise every day.'

'What if it's a nasty surprise?'

'It can't be if she's the perfect wife.'

'You're bright and breezy today,' he said with fresh resentment.

'Because you're going to be leaving here soon and I can

14

have you back at home . . . Bunnikins, have you everything you need?'

'I want the television.'

She looked across at the set on a small table.

'Everything's in either Spanish or Mallorquin,' he said angrily. 'They don't stop to think about people like me.'

'I thought there was a local station which showed the news in English?'

'Only a short news. And then it's almost all about Spain. Who's interested in what goes on in this place? . . . Get someone to fit up a dish for me and bring in our card and then I can watch some decent programmes on satellite.'

'I don't think that's possible . . .'

'What is it? You can't be bothered?'

'Bunnikins, how can you say anything so hurtful?' She sounded close to tears.

'I can't understand why you won't do it.'

'Because this room faces north and a dish has to face south.'

He swore. 'Typical! They deliberately put me in a room facing the wrong way. But they'll take my money quicker than I can hand it to them.'

'You'll soon be home and then you can watch what you want.'

He scratched the side of his stubbled cheek. 'I suppose no one's bothered to ask after me?'

'Everyone has been, and wishing you well.'

'Who's "everyone"?'

'Edna rang and said I was to give you her love; Iris was in the supermarket near the cloisters and she hopes you'll very soon be out of hospital; Cora and Clive were in the post office when I collected the mail and they asked how you were and hoped you'd soon be fighting fit.'

'She asked or he did?'

'She did, as a matter of fact.'

'That's not surprising. He wouldn't give a damn if I'd died. Supercilious bastard! You didn't tell him what was the matter with me, did you?'

'Of course I didn't. I told him and Cora the same as everyone

15

else. You've suffered severe food poisoning, but we can't work out what you ate that caused it. That's right, isn't it?'

'I suppose he can't make much out of that.'

'Oh . . . I nearly forgot. Ada rang last night to ask how you were.'

'Not like her to bother about anyone else when she's so wrapped up with that little spaghetti gigolo.'

'Why are you always so nasty about him?'

'D'you expect me to say what a fine, upstanding man he is when he lets himself be trailed around like a pet dog? It's obscene. She's three times his age.'

'But . . .' She stopped, then continued in a troubled tone: 'I thought you always said that a difference in ages doesn't matter?'

'When the man's older, it doesn't,' he said hastily. 'But it's totally different when it's the woman.'

'I suppose that's right,' she said meekly.

Twenty minutes later, she stood. 'I really must go, my darling.'

'What's the rush?'

'I wish I could stay longer, but there's a special concert on in the cloisters and you've always said we must go to that sort of thing, even if it's as boring as hell, to show the locals we've got cultural taste.'

CHAPTER 3

It was the height of summer, a time when a reasonable man accepted that stress was potentially fatal. As Alvarez made for the door of his office, the phone began to ring. He ignored it. The call might be important.

Downstairs, he passed the duty cabo, who was reading a girlie magazine, and continued through to the road. Keeping on the shade side, he made his way to the old square and the Club Llueso. The barman did not bother to ask him what he wanted, but poured a large brandy and then filled a scoop with ground coffee and fixed this into the coffee machine. Alvarez carried the glass across to a window table, sat, and sipped the brandy as he stared at the swirling crowd of tourists. A very stout woman, wearing the tightest of T-shirts and the shortest of shorts, climbed the steps up to the levelled section amidst a constant wobble of flesh.

'Fair takes the appetite away,' said the barman, as he put a cup of coffee on the table. 'D'you think she parades around like that in Berlin?'

As she reached the top, two much younger and slimmer women, equally sparsely dressed, passed her as they came down the steps. 'That's more like it,' said the barman appreciatively. 'I wouldn't mind showing them my orange trees.'

'You'd have to shed several years before they'd accept.'

'Speak for yourself.'

'I'm mature enough not to want to pluck every fruit I see.'

'You're a bloody hypocrite.' The barman left.

That was unjust, Alvarez thought. He watched the two young women until they became lost from sight and assured himself that he had admired them solely on account of the grace with which they had moved . . .

To his surprise, he found his glass was empty. He had it

17

refilled. As he drank some of the brandy, preparatory to pouring what was left into the coffee, he heard the church clock strike the hour. Time had the annoying quality of always moving at an unwanted pace; enjoy oneself and it raced, suffer and it loitered . . .

Back in his office, breathless and sweating from the climb up the stairs, the telephone rang. He picked up the receiver.

'I've been trying to get hold of you for the past hour,' a woman said angrily.

His tone became one of patient authority. 'In my job, I cannot spend my time in the office, just sitting down.'

'From all accounts, you do your best.'

'Who's talking?' he demanded.

'Concha Marti.'

She was not a woman to be treated cavalierly. 'I've only this moment returned from a very difficult and exhausting investigation.'

'I saw Dolores yesterday morning and she said you're completely out of condition. I told her, that's because, like all men, you eat and drink far too much. She should feed you on simple food, like chickpeas, and throw every bottle into the dustbin.'

The Marti family had always been regarded as peculiar, not to say downright insane. 'I am a very busy man. Do you want something?'

'Would I be talking to you if I didn't? . . . The señor's more difficult to understand than a two-year-old, so it's me doing the phoning. D'you understand?'

'You're phoning in connection with what?'

'I'm trying to tell you, aren't I? Why d'you keep interrupting?'

He hadn't interrupted her once, but he was not prepared to point that out. Not only was she an aggressive woman with a tongue edged with steel, she and Dolores were friends. 'Someone is in trouble?'

'The señora.'

'What has happened to her?'

'If he knew that, he wouldn't be going on so, would he?'

'She's missing?'

'Went out yesterday afternoon and never came back.'

'What is the señor's name?'

Her answer was a jumble of sound, and he asked her to spell out the name. Ogden. Since English pronunciation was often a mystery even to the English, he'd no better idea how to say Ogden than she had. 'Has he asked his friends if they know where she is?'

'He's been on the phone a lot. Can't understand what he says, of course.'

'Why not?'

'Sweet Mary! but you ask stupid questions. He speaks in English, that's why not.'

'Why's he asked you to phone me?'

'Haven't I said?'

'What I mean is, do you work for him?'

'Of course I do, even if they're a couple of skinflints. When I asked for nine hundred an hour instead of eight hundred, the señora tried to tell me they couldn't afford that much.' There was a snort of derision. 'She's a fool to think I would go on working for eight hundred when down in the port it's now over a thousand. And what is an extra hundred to the likes of them? You tell me that.'

'It does mount up over time . . .'

'Listen to him! It mounts up. You think a foreigner has to worry like that when they're as rich as a mayor who's enjoyed ten years of brown envelopes?'

He thought few foreigners could be that rich. 'What's the address?'

'Ca'n Nou.'

'Which is where?'

'Cami de Polso.'

In the past couple of years, reputedly at the European Union's expense – this seemed likely since the exercise had been unnecessary – every lane in the countryside had been given a name and posted; this was not one he recognized, but he was not going to give her the satisfaction of admitting so. 'Tell the señor I'll be along as soon as possible.'

Having replaced the receiver, he studied the files and paper which littered the desk and sighed at the thought of all the work involved if ever he decided to sort them out and clear them up. He checked the time. It should be possible to speak to Ogden about his missing wife before it would be necessary to stop work for lunch. Lunch. Dolores hadn't cooked Cocido Andaluz for quite a while so perhaps she was doing so now. In her hands, beef, bacon, beans, potatoes, pumpkin, chorizo, morcilla, garlic, tomatoes, and spices, became miraculously transformed into ambrosia . . . But what if the unthinkable were thought? What if Dolores had listened to Concha's ravings? Lunch then might be so plain and uninteresting that even a starving pilgrim would hesitate to eat . . . He left the room a troubled man.

Downstairs, the cabo was still reading; his resentment at Alvarez's interruption was clear. 'Never heard of the road.'

Alvarez left the post and made his way to a shop near his parked car which sold electrical goods, including computer equipment. The young woman behind the counter was too busy concentrating on a computer game – set up to attract customers' attention – to notice him, until he said: 'Do you know where Cami de Polso is?'

'No.' She zapped a couple of aliens.

'Where's the boss?'

'Couldn't say.'

'Would you see if he's around?'

She zapped a couple more. 'Why?'

'Because I want a word with him. Cuerpo General de Policia.'

'And there was me thinking you was Arnie!' She reluctantly left, to go around a display of television sets into the back of the shop.

He wondered who Arnie was. Having watched which controls she'd used, he set out to zap the oncoming aliens. He failed ingloriously and a notice came up on screen to tell him he'd been eliminated.

A voice from behind him said: 'You need to be under twenty to survive.'

He had known Valverde long enough to remember a skinny, snot-nosed boy from a family so poor that he had always worn cast-off clothing. Now he was sleekly plump and dressed in the height of casual fashion. They shook hands. Valverde, uncertain why Alvarez wanted to speak to him – the assistant had not bothered to explain – and therefore fearing it might be the wish to buy a piece of equipment at a heavy discount, complained about the rise in the cost of living, the drop in the numbers of tourists and the miserly spending of those who did arrive, and the rapacity of the tax collector who was rapidly reducing him to penury.

'It's a cruel world,' Alvarez agreed. 'You own a lot of property about the place, don't you?'

Valverde, ever careful, said: 'Just the odd field, bought for old times' sake seeing as the old folks used to farm.'

'Then you may know where Cami de Polso is?'

'That's what you want to know?'

'Yes.'

He prepared to be more helpful. 'Can't say I've ever come across the road, but there are so many new names these days it's impossible to keep up with 'em.'

'Maybe you've dealt with the bloke who lives in a house along there – Señor Ogden?'

'We've certainly done business with a foreigner called something like that.'

'Tell me what his house is named and I'll know if it's the man I'm after.'

'Can't give it offhand, but he bought a video and Julio fitted that, so it'll be in the records. I'll have a look.'

He was gone less than two minutes. 'Ca'n Nou.'

'That's the place. How do I get there?'

'Take the old road to Playa Neuva. Four to five kilometres along there's a property been bought by a foreigner with too much money and he's had all the stone walls rebuilt and added a pair of wrought-iron gates that wouldn't disgrace a castle. Just past there, turn left and carry on for a couple of kilometres. Julio says it's a new villa, on its own and close to the road.'

'I thought all around there had been declared a conservation area and so no building was allowed?'

'What a droll man you can be.' Valverde patted Alvarez on the arm.

21

CHAPTER 4

Alvarez turned off the Playa Neuva road into a lane that twisted and turned like a snake in torment. He slowed, from choice as well as necessity. Here, despite its nearness to the coast, was the true Mallorca, preserved because foreigners were interested only in the froth of life. Here were sheep and goats, figs preparing to ripen, stubble that marked crops harvested and stored . . .

As he rounded a bend, a nameboard listing Ca'n Nou came into sight. He braked to a halt and looked across a field to see a large, newly built villa. The true Mallorca, at least beyond the mountains, could exist only in a nostalgic mind, he told himself sourly. Foreigners had money and money corrupted the past as well as the present and the future.

He drove up the dirt track and came to a halt in front of the house. As he stepped out on to the gravel, the door opened and a man came out, eyes puckered to counter the glare of the sun. Middle to late sixties, Alvarez judged; beginning to bald, noticeably overweight, heavily featured face showing signs of ill health. He said in English: 'Señor Ogden? My name is Inspector Alvarez. Your maid rang me at the post to say your wife is missing . . .'

'There's no sign of her. What can have happened? Where is she?'

'Perhaps I might enter?'

Ogden stepped to one side and Alvarez went past him and into the hall. Two doors led off this and one was open to show a large sitting-room, colourfully decorated and luxuriously furnished. Since Ogden made no further move, Alvarez went through. The room was cool, thanks to air conditioning. 'Señor, I will need to ask you questions, but first I should

22

like to see a photograph of your wife – can you provide me with one?'

Ogden left. When he returned, he handed across a photograph. Alvarez studied this. Sabrina was clearly very much younger than her husband. Significant? She had an oval face, long blonde hair, blue eyes, a pert nose, a sensuously formed mouth, and a shapely body – few men would look at her with neutral thoughts. 'May I keep this for a while, señor?'

'If you must.'

'I will take great care of it.' He sat and after a moment, Ogden did the same. 'Will you tell me exactly what has happened recently, remembering that something unusual that occurred even days ago may be significant.'

Ogden spoke disjointedly. He'd been very weak since returning from hospital and had spent every afternoon in bed. The previous day, after lunch, Sabrina had come into the bedroom to say she was going out for some fresh air. He'd heard her drive off in her car. He'd read for a very short while, then drifted off to sleep. When he'd got up, it was to find she had not returned home.

'Did that worry you?'

'Not really. It was getting on, but I just thought she'd either lost count of the time or stopped off to see a friend.'

'When did you begin to worry?'

'I suppose as it got later and later and she still didn't turn up.'

'Did you phone all your friends to see if she was with them?'

'I . . . No.'

'Why not?'

There was a long pause. 'She believes marriage is all about trust. I didn't want her to think I was checking up on her.'

'But surely you were far more concerned for her safety than what she might think?'

'Yes. Only in the end . . . I couldn't.'

'Couldn't what?'

'Phone.'

'Why not?'

'I'd had a drink or two to calm myself down so . . .'

In the end, he'd become too calm to phone. Could the photograph, Alvarez wondered, explain the otherwise inexplicable – a man who was worried by his wife's disappearance, yet instead of doing all he could to find her, drank himself silly? 'When did you recover consciousness?'

Ogden mumbled: 'In the morning, just before Concha arrived.'

'Did you then phone your friends?'

'Well, of course I did,' he answered, with a pathetic attempt at indignation.

'The señora left here in her car. Presumably, you've no idea where that is now?'

'How could I?'

'What is the make, colour, and registration number?'

'It's a green BMW. I can't remember the number.'

'Are the papers in the house?'

'We were told we had to keep them in the car . . . What's happened to her?'

'You have no idea?'

'D'you think I'd just be sitting here if I did?'

'Is it possible that she might be staying away of her own will?'

'What kind of a suggestion is that?'

'The relations between you are not under any kind of a strain?'

'We couldn't be happier.'

'You told me you'd recently been in hospital – what were you suffering from?'

'Very severe food poisoning.'

'What had you eaten to give you that?'

'I don't know.'

'Was your wife ill?'

'No.'

'So she visited you in hospital?'

'Of course she did. Every day. And stayed for as long as she possibly could.'

Ogden had spoken with such emphasis that Alvarez was reminded of the old Mallorquin saying, If a man swears too

24

loudly that he has not seen your missing lamb, look first in his stew pot.

Back home, Alvarez walked through the front room, used only on very formal occasions, into the next one that was both sitting- and dining-room. Jaime was seated at the table, a bottle of brandy, a bowl of ice, and a glass in front of him. Alvarez leaned across to open the right-hand door of the Mallorquin sideboard, brought out a glass, sat. Jaime pushed the brandy and ice across.

'Any idea what's for grub?' Alvarez asked, as he poured himself a generous brandy.

'She's not said anything.'

He savoured the faint aroma that was creeping through the bead curtain. 'Doesn't smell like chickpeas.' He added three cubes of ice to the brandy.

'I should bloody well hope not! If she tried to give us that sort of muck, I'd have something to say –' Jaime realized he'd been speaking quite loudly and he came to an abrupt stop, stared uneasily at the bead curtain. Dolores did not appear to ask him to tell her exactly what he would say. He relaxed. 'What the hell makes you think she might be?'

'Concha Marti told her that if we were out of condition, she ought to feed us on simple food like chickpeas and throw every bottle out of the house.'

'The whole family are just troublemakers . . . Bruno – he's married to Concha's sister – says that after living with her, hell will be heaven. Why be so stupid as to have anything to do with any of 'em?'

'She rang the post to say she works for an English family and the wife's vanished.'

'Any idea what's going on?'

'He must be more than twice her age, he's pot-bellied, and he's balding.'

'She's taken off with someone else?'

'Wouldn't you?'

The bead curtain swished as Dolores came through from the kitchen. She was perspiring freely and her dress was creased and stained, yet she still possessed the haughty air of superiority that falsely suggested Andaluce ancestry. 'Ha!'

They stared at her, not understanding the significance of that exclamation, yet nervously certain it would reflect to their disadvantage.

'So! Even the most foolish of men can finally open his eyes to the truth!'

'What are you on about?' Jaime muttered.

'Is it not so obvious that even you can understand?'

He felt the need of a drink, but his glass was empty and this clearly was not the moment to refill it.

'My cousin,' she said with deep satisfaction, 'has opened his eyes.'

Jaime was relieved to discover that he was not involved in whatever was going on.

'He has learned that when a man is old, his stomach proclaims his love of excess, and his hair disappears, he becomes a clown when he lusts after young women.'

'I am not old . . .' Alvarez began indignantly.

'Very soon, middle age will no longer be a stranger.'

'My stomach is almost flat . . .'

'If you were a woman, this house would be shamed.'

'My hair's thick . . .'

'No thicker than the leaves on a shade tree in a winter storm.'

'And I do not lust after young women . . .'

'Let a twenty-year-old foreigner so much as smile at you and your wits vanish.' She turned and swept back into the kitchen.

Alvarez morosely finished his drink, poured himself another. Since Adam, it had been the fate of man to be misunderstood by woman.

The heat, more intense than ever, was not conducive to work. Even though he'd enjoyed a siesta, Alvarez's eyelids were heavy as he finally reached the office. He sat, mopped his face and neck with a handkerchief, relaxed . . .

The phone woke him.

'My name is Señora Shaw,' said a woman, speaking laboured,

heavily accented Spanish. 'Señor Ogden says why you have not spoken to him?'

'I'm afraid I don't understand,' he replied in English.

'Why not?' she snapped in Spanish.

He pictured her as skinny, beak-nosed, and critical of everything Spanish. He continued to speak in English, happy to be as pig-headed as she. 'I am not certain why he should expect me to be in touch with him until there is something to report.'

'Do you say that . . . that . . .' She struggled to find the words in Spanish.

'Perhaps if you said it in English, señora?'

Her tone was bitter. 'Have you not learned anything about Señora Ogden's whereabouts?'

'I fear not. But you may rest assured that everything possible is being done. Are you a friend of the señor and señora?'

'I am acquainted with them.'

'Then you may be able to help me.'

'Most unlikely.'

'Nevertheless, I should like to meet and speak to you.'

'You obviously haven't understood me.'

'Señora, you may think you cannot help, but it is possible you possess knowledge the significance of which you cannot appreciate since you do not have all the facts. Will it be possible for me to visit your house in half an hour's time?'

'If you must,' she answered bad-temperedly.

'May I have your address?'

That call completed, he rang Traffic and asked them to check the records to find out what was the registration number of the green BMW belonging to Señora Sabrina Ogden, who lived at Ca'n Nou, Cami de Polso, Llueso. His request caused much resentment. The computer system was set up to identify the owner of a car from the registration number, not vice versa, and it would take endless time and trouble to do as he was asking . . .

As he replaced the receiver, he thought with scorn that the staff in Traffic were a bunch of layabouts.

CHAPTER 5

Alvarez eventually found parking space for his car, then walked, through a drifting swirl of tourists, to the block of flats, built only a few years before, that fronted the pedestrian path which skirted the bay's edge. He checked the list of names by the entryphone, pressed the button for Mrs N. Shaw.

'Yes?'

The small speaker had made her sound even more autocratic and crabby than had the phone. 'Inspector Alvarez, señora,' he said despondently. The door lock buzzed.

The foyer was marble lined with one wall made of looking glass so that the area appeared to be double its real size; there was a small collection of cacti in the recess under the stairs. The lift was panelled and thickly carpeted. It was all a far cry from the fisherman's cottage which had previously occupied the site.

The door of flat 4a was opened by a woman who bore little physical resemblance to his mental picture of her. She was not thin, but well formed, her face was fine boned and attractive, and her dress casually smart. But he had not been so wrong as to her character. After thanking her for her kindness in agreeing to speak to him, she said, 'A sheer waste of time,' with arrogant certainty.

'I hope . . .'

'Don't just stand there; come on in.'

The large sitting-room was expensively furnished in the impeccable but icy taste of a glossy magazine. Most of the bay was visible through the large picture window, and he came to a stop in the centre of the Chinese carpet. 'Isn't it a wonderful view! And at night, when the moon's out and reflected on the water, it's magical!' His enthusiasm made him speak quickly.

'It's quite attractive if one hasn't travelled extensively.'

Why was it that life so often bestowed its gifts on those who hadn't the wit to enjoy them, whilst denying those who had?

She sat. 'Please be as quick as possible.'

It seemed that she expected him to remain standing – cap in hand, had he been wearing one. He sat. She was from the past. Before the tourist invasion, the English who had visited or lived on the island had almost all been from relatively wealthy backgrounds. They had been polite, but seldom bothered to hide their sense of social and intellectual superiority. Yet this attitude had not aroused a tithe of the resentment that their successors had amassed. More than most, Spaniards respected honour and the foreigners' honour could never be impugned because it rested on their superiority. It was from such period had come the expression, still occasionally spoken by an older man when he wanted to impress the sanctity of his promise, 'On the word of an Englishman' . . .

'Did you hear what I said?'

He hurriedly brought his mind back to the present. 'Señora, since it was you whom Señor Ogden asked to phone me, you must know him and his wife very well?'

'He called on me for help because I speak Spanish.'

He would have liked to disillusion her.

'This is a small expatriate community and therefore inevitably one meets most members of it, whether or not one seeks to do so.'

'When Señora Ogden failed to return home, her husband first thought she was visiting friends. Would you know if she did indeed do so?'

'I have no idea.'

'Do they have many friends?'

'That is a question for them, not me.'

'If you were to describe their marriage, would you call it a happy one?'

'I consider it a gross impertinence to concern oneself with other people's relationships.'

'Regretfully, a policeman frequently has no choice but to do just that. I need to understand the truth of their relationship

29

if I am to discover whether something serious may have happened to the señora, or it is more probable that her disappearance is at her own wish. Señor Ogden showed me a photograph of her and this made it clear that she is very much younger than he. In such a marriage, there can be unusual stresses and strains.' Dolores would have had something to say about that observation had she heard it! 'Would you think the relationship between Señor Ogden and Señora Ogden had become troubled?'

'I hoped I had made it perfectly clear that I do not concern myself with such questions.'

'Perhaps for once you would, señora.'

'Why should I?'

'From certain things Señor Ogden told me, it seemed the relationship between him and his wife might indeed have become difficult. If that is so, the fact is important since it might well explain what has happened. So if you would . . .'

'There is no point in continuing.'

'I do have one or two more questions.'

'Please be kind enough to leave.'

He left.

He poured himself another brandy. 'Is there any ice left?'

Jaime tilted the container until he could look inside. 'Yeah.' He pushed it across.

Alvarez picked out three cubes and dropped them into his glass. 'I've had one hell of a day!'

'No worse than mine.'

'Have you had to try to question a real dragon of a woman?'

'You call that work?' He finished his drink. 'Shove the bottle over . . . Has the missing wife turned up yet?'

'There's no sign of her. And I reckon she won't be surfacing in a hurry because she's taken off with someone else.' Alvarez's tone became reflective. 'You know, foreigners lead busy lives.'

'You mean, lucky lives!'

The bead curtains parted as Dolores swept through to come to a halt facing the table, hands on her hips. 'Foreigners are lucky because they lead lives of disgrace? So! In his secret mind, my husband envies them and yearns for the chance to follow their example!'

Jaime looked to Alvarez for help, failed to find it.

CHAPTER 6

Alvarez sat at his desk, searched amongst the litter of papers and files for the unopened letter on the back of which he'd written Ogden's telephone number. He found it, dialled.

'Have you found her?' was Ogden's immediate response.

'I'm sorry, señor, no, I have not.'

'Something terrible's happened to her.'

'You do not think she might have wished to disappear?'

'For God's sake, why would she do such a thing?'

'There could be more than one reason.'

'If she'd known what was going to happen, she'd have told me.'

'It is my experience that when people are worried, or something unusual happens to them, they do not always do as one might expect . . . I need to talk to your friends to discover if any of them can tell me something that would help. Would you give me their names and addresses, especially those whom you believe to be close to the señora.'

He wrote, frequently having to ask the other to spell out a name so that he could be certain he had noted it correctly.

Ca'n Ximor was an urbanizacíon, five kilometres inland from Llueso, set in an area of pine woods. Because this had been a noted area for a rare species of crossbills, an attempt had been made to block the proposed development but, as always, commercialism had overriden the demands of conservation. Because of the distance from the sea, it was not popular with people seeking holiday homes and many of the plots had yet to sell. The developers' misfortune was the inhabitants' fortune – there was an unusual sense of peace.

Alvarez slowed and turned into the short drive which led to the garage of the bungalow at the end of the spur road.

He stepped out of the car, crossed to the three steps which led down to the panelled wooden door, rang the bell. There was no immediate response and when, at the edge of his vision, he saw movement in the butano-coloured bougain-villaea to his right, he climbed back up the steps to try to identify what had moved. After a moment, he made out the green form of a praying mantis which had frozen into immobility.

The front door was opened by Keane, who wore bathing trunks. 'Hullo, there.'

Alvarez returned down the steps.

'I am Inspector Alvarez of the Cuerpo General de Policia.'

'No doubt here in connection with the disappearance of Sabrina?'

'You have heard about that?'

'A never-to-be-repeated confidence is one that takes twenty-four hours to travel from east to west . . . Come along in.' As Alvarez stepped into the small hall, he said: 'Is it too early to offer you a drink?'

'As we say, If it is too early to drink, the cock has not yet made its first crow.'

'Small wonder we choose to live here! What will you have?'

'A coñac with just ice, please.'

'Carry on through to the patio.' Keane pointed to an opened doorway.

Alvarez walked through the comfortably furnished sitting-room and out on to the covered patio. He sat on one of the chairs grouped around a table, stared at the pool, the rough garden, the pine trees, and the not-so-distant hills.

Keane came out, a tray in his hands. He put two glasses on the table, sat, picked up the nearer glass. 'Here's wishing you health, wealth, and cocks that always crow well before dawn.' He drank. 'I presume from the fact that you're here now, Sabrina has not reappeared?'

'She hasn't, no.'

'My wife's shopping in Llueso and she said she'd try and call in at their place to see if there's anything she can do to help. Inevitably, of course, the offer's of little real practical value. What can one do except utter the usual vapid hopes with all the sincerity one can muster?'

'Can you suggest where Señora Ogden might be?'

Keane held the glass in his right hand and jiggled it so that the ice began to revolve, repeatedly bumping into the sides. 'Any suggestion from me would be wild speculation.'

'How well do you know Señor and Señora Ogden?'

'An impossible question to answer. Can one ever really know another person well? Even a close friend can suddenly do or say something totally unexpected.'

'Perhaps, though, you can judge whether there might be difficulties in their relationship?'

'Show me a relationship that's free of them.'

'When speaking to Señor Ogden, I gained the impression that it's possible all may not be well between his wife and him.'

'Impressions have a habit of being very misleading.'

'You have heard no rumours to that effect?'

'I try never to listen to rumours. They're so inclined to arouse expectations which aren't fulfilled.'

'Señor, you seem to be careful not to answer my questions directly.'

'As a detective, surely that's a familiar problem?'

'My inquiries are solely directed to discovering whether anything unfortunate has happened to the señora. If it becomes clear she has disappeared of her own free will, then I am no longer concerned and everything I have learned will be forgotten.'

'An admirable sense of discretion.'

'Have there been rumours concerning Señor and Señora Ogden?'

'Rumours are like miracles. You have to believe in them before you believe in them.'

'You still have not answered me.'

'You are a man of persistence!' Keane drank, replaced the glass on the table. 'And I am a man who acknowledges that there are times when one has to accede to the demands of public duty . . . Some time ago – around the beginning of February, at a guess – an inveterate rumourmonger, best described as a rough diamond since he doesn't sparkle until he's well cut, was full of the story that Sabrina had become very friendly with a man of approximately her own age.'

'Was the man named?'

'He was.'

'Who is he?'

'Rino Ruffolo.'

'Do you know him?'

'I have met him at parties.'

'Where does he live?'

'In Parelona.'

'He is a wealthy man?'

'He was plucked off the back streets of Naples by Ada, who took a fancy to him.'

'Are you suggesting he is a gigolo?'

'The term originally meant a professional dancing partner and I credit Ada with just enough sense not to have taken to the floor in years. Toy boy is the modern expression.'

'Is he younger than this lady?'

'It would be ungallant to compute the difference.'

'Do you think there is truth in the rumour?'

'Life shows that when a man is very much older than his wife, he must possess great charm, unusual power, or considerable wealth to retain her affection. Whether Bevis's wealth is sufficient, I rather doubt.'

The sky was cloudless, the sea a millpond; as the road twisted and turned, views, some dramatic, some softer edged, opened up and disappeared; the trees and undergrowth offered an infinite range of greens and browns. Enraptured by so much beauty, Alvarez forgot to be terrified by the dangerous drops that repeatedly edged the road.

He caught a brief glimpse of the long, low, white building that was the Parelona Hotel, the epitome of quiet luxury. He could not remember its being built, but there were a few in the village who could. Then, there had been no road and all men and materials had had to be transported either by boat or mule. On the opening night, a fleet of boats had been hired to take invited guests there and to return those who were not staying. For years afterwards, that event had been remembered with awe by the villagers because briefly they had been touched by the world of riches.

It was now the age of the common man, but the area remained one of privilege, although in one respect this was qualified. Because the land around the hotel and on the surrounding hills was very expensive, and the cost of building was much greater than elsewhere, only the wealthy could afford to own the property; unfortunately, the Spanish law did not allow private beaches, and so during the summer buses and ferries brought tourists to the long crescent of sand and the crystal-clear water and they, naturally lacking the mannered restraint which wealth induced, tended to be noisy and often indecorous in their behaviour. However, such hoi polloi stayed in the kind of hotel where one could not eat when one chose, but had to do so at times dictated, and so by early evening they would all have departed. Then, the residents could once more enjoy the exclusivity for which they had paid so dearly.

Ca Na Ada was a very large, ranch-style villa, set in a garden filled with colour. As he climbed out of the car, Alvarez heard the tinkling of water and he looked to his right and saw, beyond a palm tree, a stone fountain with a metre-high jet. Since most of the water had to be piped from the port, it was expensive; a fountain eventually lost a considerable proportion of the water that passed through it . . . He shook his head. If he lived to be a hundred, he would never understand the foreigners' stupidity in failing to realize that a peseta not spent was a peseta in the pocket.

He crossed to the front door and rang the bell. The door was opened by a man in white jacket, black tie, and striped trousers, into whose expression there slipped a measure of contempt as he surveyed Alvarez's somewhat dishevelled appearance. 'Yes?'

'Cuerpo General de Policia,' Alvarez snapped.

The man's expression blanked.

'Is Señor Ruffolo here?'

'He is at home.'

'I want to talk to him.'

He was shown into a sitting-room that had a floor area not far short of the whole of the downstairs of his own home. It had been furnished and decorated seemingly with little regard to taste, and because of the vivid colours the first impression was of sheer vulgarity; then, a calmer inspection revealed individual pieces of furniture that were of unmistakable quality which seemed to raise the question, how could someone both lack and possess a sense of beauty? Since the view was nature made, that provoked no such problem. There were three sliding windows and through them could be seen, above the hedge, the bay, headlands, and open sea . . .

As a door opened, he turned.

Ruffolo crossed to the nearer settee and settled on it, one arm trailing along its back. 'You want something?' he asked, in fluent if heavily accented Spanish.

Only Italy, Alvarez thought, could produce a tall, slender, curly-headed man, almost as handsome as he so obviously thought himself, whose movements were touched with feminine grace, who could wear a heavy gold medallion on a thick gold chain and a large, gem-studded signet ring without even a trace of doubt. 'I should like to ask you some questions.'

'Have I been driving too fast on the autoroute?'

'I expect so; most people do . . . Do you know Señora Ogden?'

'Who?'

'Señora Sabrina Ogden.'

'No one ever mentions surnames. Yes, I know Sabrina. Why d'you ask?'

'Perhaps you've not heard that she's disappeared?'

'Really.'

'You are not concerned?'

'What is more natural than that she should decide to leave her senile husband?'

'I didn't say she'd disappeared voluntarily.'

'What alternative is there?'

'I'm here to find out. What emotional state has she been in recently?'

'I have no idea.' Ruffolo leaned across to open the heavily chased silver cigarette case on the small occasional table by the side of the settee. He lit a cigarette.

'Are you a friend of hers?'

'I have met her, no more.'

'An Englishman has told me that at the beginning of this year you were very friendly with her.'

'The English are all so frustrated that they have only to see a man speaking to a woman with a measure of admiration and they conjure up an affair.'

'When did you last talk to her?'

'At some party, or other. How can I remember? We go to so many parties.'

'Do you have a girlfriend?'

'What sort of a question is that supposed to be? I live here with my beloved Ada.'

'Are you friendly with another woman?'

'The question is insulting.'

The second of the inner doors opened and Ada swept into

the room. She came to a stop and stared at Alvarez. 'Carlos told me you're a detective?' She spoke in English, careless he might not understand her.

'That is so, señora.'

'Señorita.'

'My apologies.'

'You don't look like a detective.'

She didn't look like a rich woman. She was fat in the wrong places; her face was lined and rough; her hair had been dyed a strange shade of orange; her heavy make-up had been inexpertly applied; her dress fitted only where it touched; she wore jewellery that mocked instead of complementing because it was elegant.

'What do you want here?'

Ruffolo spoke quickly in English that was more Bronx than BBC. 'He's asking me questions.'

'About what?' She sat down heavily on one of the chairs and her very full skirt briefly flared out to reveal expanses of flabby flesh.

'He says Sabrina's vanished.'

She turned to Alvarez. 'That's fact?'

'Indeed, señorita. She left her home on Sunday afternoon and has not been seen since.'

'Why should you think Rino can help find her?'

He was about to answer, but was interrupted. Rino said: 'Some idiot Englishman has told him I've been friendly with her.' He laughed. 'As if I could find pleasure in the company of a woman so lacking in taste as to marry a man old enough to be her grandfather.'

'That's good reason for her to want to wander,' she said sharply.

Rino came gracefully to his feet, crossed to her chair, took one of her hands in both of his and stared intently into her eyes. 'My angel, do I hear the whisper of a question? Could Rino have been friendly with her, but does not wish to admit this? Such a question is like a dagger to my heart.'

'Men can't keep their eyes off her.'

'Because they have English wives who believe that it is a sin to enjoy the pleasures of the flesh. But would I stare at another woman when I have my Ada who knows that to enjoy the pleasures of the flesh is to live like a god?'

'You mustn't say things like that in front of a stranger,' she simpered.

'Not tell the world I am the luckiest man alive?' He gently disengaged his hands, turned to face Alvarez. 'In ancient times in my country, a man who spread malicious gossip had his tongue torn out. The Englishman who said this should have his tongue eaten by sewer rats.' He brought an embroidered silk handkerchief from his pocket and dabbed his forehead. 'I am on fire with anger.'

'Then have a swim and cool down,' she said.

'I don't think so.'

'Suit yourself, but I want a word with the inspector so vamoose for a while.'

He hesitated, then crossed to the inner door, his resentment obvious.

She waited until he'd gone to say to Alvarez: 'All right, let's hear the rest.'

'The rest of what, señorita?' Alvarez replied.

'Who's the bastard who said Rino was having it off with Sabrina?'

'I do not know his identity.'

'Bullshit!' Her tone became scornful. 'Shocked you, have I?'

'Of course not,' he protested weakly.

'Who was he?'

'Señorita, surely you understand that in any police inquiry there is information which has to remain confidential?'

'Yeah? Then at least you can tell me why the bastard said it?'

'I do not know why.'

'There's more you don't know than you do.'

The superior chief would agree with that, he thought. She had not managed to hide the fact that behind the pugnacity was a measure of uncertainty. 'My informant mentioned the rumour; he did not try to suggest there was any truth in it.'

'And that was enough to have you come here, shouting dirt?'

'It was my duty to learn whether there could be any truth in the story.'

'And now you know it's crap.'

'I wonder why someone would wish to be so cruel?'

'Because most of the expats haven't anything better to do than slag somebody and it's twice as much fun to slag me.'

'Why should that be?'

She didn't answer the question, but said: 'You know who I reckon it was?'

'Tell me, señorita.'

'Someone who made a try for her and got turned down flat. There's nothing gets a man more vindictive than a sharp brush-off.'

'If that were so, why should he name Señor Ruffolo?'

'Because Rino's Italian; and because whoever it was is small-minded and intensely jealous of anyone who enjoys life.'

'Can you suggest who this person might be?'

'Anyone not yet in a zimmer frame.'

'Suppose you're right and inventing this rumour was an act of vindictiveness – do you think it's possible that she has in truth been having an affair?'

'What's more likely? Bevis is a pompous prat and it'll be a long time since his performance matched his ambition. There's nothing so off-putting to a woman as a floundering man . . . D'you want a drink?'

The change of subject was so abrupt that it was a while before Alvarez responded. 'That would be a pleasure, señorita.'

'What d'you want?'

'Might I have a coñac with just ice?'

'It's liberty hall.'

No doubt until one's wishes ran counter to hers. He watched her pick up from the table by her side what looked like a television remote control. She pressed the single button on it.

She answered his unspoken question. 'Carlos tried telling me he couldn't hear me call him, so I bought something that lets him know loud and clear when I want him.' She put the control down. 'Where are you from?'

'I live in Llueso.'

'Are you married?'

Before he could answer, the inner door opened and Carlos stepped into the room.

'The usual for me,' Ada said. 'And brandy with just ice for the inspector.'

Carlos left.

She jerked her thumb in the direction of the door. 'His previous job was with a couple who reckoned they were God's gift to high society. He started here by telling me how things should be done. Soon learned he did 'em my way or he started walking.'

That did not surprise him. She ran her life as she wanted it run.

'You didn't say if you're married?'

'I'm not.'

'Why not at your age? One of them, are you?'

He was amused, not annoyed, by her personal questions. 'Many years ago, I was engaged. But my fiancée was killed in an accident before we could marry.'

'And you've not met anyone else to take her place?'

'Sadly, no,' he answered, knowing this to be a lie, but not prepared to admit that usually it had not been he who had drawn back.

'I once had a young man. He wasn't killed in an accident.'

He was convinced that her cryptic comment hid memories as painful as were his of Juana-María . . .

Carlos returned, carrying a large silver salver on which was a bottle of champagne in a cooler, a bottle of brandy, a small ice container, a flute, and a glass; he put the champagne and flute down on the table by Ada's chair, the brandy, ice, and glass on the one by Alvarez's. He left.

'He can't stand giving people the bottle to help themselves.'

'Which is precisely why you do it?'

She filled her flute, drank.

Alvarez drove with very great care as he crossed the bridge over the torrente to enter the village; such great care that the

42

driver of the Mondeo behind him hooted in angry frustration. 'Roadhog,' he said loudly.

Once over the bridge, and even though there was little room, the Mondeo drew abreast and the driver shook his fist. Alvarez raised one finger in the unmistakable gesture of contempt and this provoked such fury that the other driver momentarily lost concentration and had to brake violently to avoid a crash with one of the parked cars. Alvarez was still laughing when he drew up in front of home.

He was surprised to find the family seated around the dining-table. Speaking with care, he said: 'Am I a little late?'

'Are you a little late?' Dolores spoke histrionically. 'You can ask that when, because I insist some of us show manners, we have had to wait for your return before we ate; wait so long that in the end we could wait no longer. But by then, the meal, over which I slaved the whole morning, was ruined.'

Typically, Jaime chose the wrong moment to try to soothe his wife's feelings. 'It wasn't ruined. I thought it was delicious.'

'To a deaf man, all languages are the same.'

Alvarez said: 'I was unavoidably detained . . .'

'In a bar.'

'In Parelona. I had to go there . . .' He had to sit down. He collapsed on to his chair. 'I had to make inquiries.'

Jaime said: 'About the woman who's married to a husband twice her age and is having it off with – '

'Be quiet!' snapped Dolores. 'Try to remember you have children who are not yet old enough to understand the true character of their father.' She spoke once more to Alvarez. 'It took you all morning and half the afternoon to question a woman?'

'There was her boyfriend as well. And I have to admit, we did have a drink, or two.'

'More like four or five,' said Juan precociously.

For once, Dolores did not rebuke her son's rudeness. 'No doubt she is a foreigner?'

'She's English. But if you're thinking . . .'

'My thoughts come from bitter experience. But not even

that has prepared me for the shame of learning that my cousin lusts after a married woman.'

'You're mixing everything up. Don't you see . . .'

'I only wish I could not. If the good Lord were kind, he would blind me to your behaviour. Truly it is said that only the grave can still a man's stupidity.'

Only a monastery could grant a living man peace.

CHAPTER 8

Alvarez parked his car and crossed to the three steps and the front door, rang the bell. As he waited, he studied the bougainvillaea, curious to note if a praying mantis were still there.

The door was opened and he faced a woman who immediately evoked in his mind the image of a fading flower. 'Señora Keane?'

'Yes?'

He introduced himself and asked if her husband was at home.

'Are you here again because of Sabrina?'

'Yes, I am.'

'There's still no news of her?'

'I am afraid not.'

'Oh!' After a moment, she said: 'I'm so sorry, leaving you standing there, only I was thinking how awful . . . Please do come in.'

He followed her through the house to the patio. Keane, who had been swimming, stood up halfway along the pool, the water up to his chest. 'I didn't hear the cock crow, but then my hearing is no doubt less acute than yours.'

'This is Inspector Alvarez . . .' she began, flustered by her husband's facetiousness.

'Introductions are unnecessary.' He ploughed through the water, leaving a trail of eddies, and climbed the steps. He bent down and picked up a towel.

'Sabrina's still missing,' she said.

He dried his face and neck. 'So I presumed from this unexpected visit . . . Inspector, come and sit in the shade and tell me what precisely brings you back here while my wife pours drinks.'

They settled on patio chairs after telling Cora what they would like; she went into the house.

'When I was here before,' Alvarez said, 'you mentioned the rumour that Señora Ogden had become very friendly with Señor Ruffolo.'

'True.'

'You would not tell me the name of the person who had told you this. Would you do so now, please?'

'Why?'

'I want to find out if he originated the rumour.'

'That's very unlikely. He was a highly successful business-man, which means he has a limited imagination except when it comes to benefiting himself at the expense of others.'

'Nevertheless, I wish to question him.'

'You have my assurance that the experience would be far from enlightening.'

'Will you give me his name?'

'I think not. He's not a close friend so there'd be small pleasure in betraying him.'

'I wonder, señor, if you refuse because no such person exists?'

'Now that's an odd thing to say!'

'It is difficult to understand why you should not name the person if you do not have a valid reason for not doing so.'

'I think that could be called a negative suggestion.'

'A reason you wish to conceal.'

'Would you care to surmise what that might be?'

'That it was you who initiated the rumour and you did so as an act of revenge.'

'Well I'll be damned!'

'You probably were a long time ago,' Cora said with rare spirit as she came through the doorway, a tray in her hands. She put the tray down on the glass-topped bamboo table, passed one glass to Alvarez, another to her husband, lifted the third and put the tray on the floor, sat.

'Aren't you curious to know why I'm damned?' Keane asked her.

She didn't answer.

'The inspector thinks I offered a game of you-show-me-yours-and-I'll-show-you-mine with Sabrina and she flatly refused. That I started the rumour about her and Rino out of pique.'

She said with sudden force: 'That's utterly ridiculous!' She spoke more calmly to Alvarez. 'You surely can't seriously believe Clive ever chased after Sabrina?'

'It is just one of many possibilities I have to consider.'

'I know I can trust my husband implicitly.'

'Then you are to be envied, señora.' Alvarez turned to Keane. 'What surer judgement can there be? . . . Nevertheless, I still have to ask if you have often met Señora Ogden?'

'Of course. At parties.'

'Always in the company of her husband?'

'Where she goes, there goes he. Whether from pride of possession or fear of the potentials, I've no idea.'

'Have you ever met her when both of you have been on your own?'

'Is that possible? If we're both on our own, we surely can't have met?'

'You know what he means,' Cora said urgently.

'Yes. My apologies, Inspector. I freely admit to the deadly eighth sin, that of occasionally becoming pedantic. To answer your question more reasonably: I can't remember meeting her in the absence of a companion, but it has to be likely that we've bumped into each other in shops. However, the shelves of a supermarket do not induce a sense of desire in anyone but a glutton.'

'I wish you wouldn't talk like that,' his wife said.

Alvarez drained his glass, stood.

'Leaving before you've had the other half?' Keane asked.

'Regretfully, I must return to work.'

'More rumours to investigate? What an exasperating life you must lead, pursuing not the uneatable, but the uncatchable.'

Alvarez said goodbye. Keane remained seated, but Cora accompanied him to the front door. 'You must understand,' she said, speaking very quickly, 'Clive will say things without thinking how they sound to someone who doesn't know him. It really is impossible that he ever chased after Sabrina. We're far too happy for him to do something like that.'

'Then you are to be congratulated as well as envied, señora.'

As he settled behind the wheel of his car, he thought that perhaps her insistent manner, so clearly uncharacteristic, had been occasioned by the fear that her husband would find little difficulty and even less reluctance in being unfaithful to her.

Alvarez looked at his watch and with a sense of disbelief saw that only twelve minutes had passed from when he had last checked the time; one hour and eighteen minutes remained before he could leave the office and return home. He slumped back in the chair, all too conscious of a thumping head and a mouth that tasted to be beyond its sell-by date. He should not have refilled his glass quite so often. Yet it would have appeared rude if, as he reminisced with Pedro about the years since they'd last met, he had sat in front of an empty glass.

Ada Heron intrigued him. He was convinced she possessed a sharp intelligence, yet she allowed Ruffolo to reduce her to simpering stupidity. And why did she take so little care over her personal appearance? Was this ignorance or a deliberate one-finger gesture? . . .

The phone interrupted his wandering thoughts. He dragged himself upright and reached across the desk, lifted the receiver.

'Traffic. It's been one hell of a job tracking down the reg-istration number.'

What number was the idiot talking about?

'Are you still there?'

He wasn't going anywhere. 'Someone came in and needed something in a real hurry and I had to show him where it is.'

'The jefe's muttering about sending your department a special invoice for the time it's taken.'

'Is he likely to?'

'God alone knows what he'll do and maybe even He isn't smart enough to guess . . . Are you ready?'

He wrote down the registration number he was given,

thanked the caller, said goodbye, replaced the receiver. Only then did he finally remember why he had requested the number.

He slumped back in the chair. Until now he had not bothered to make a report because there were so few facts and little angered the superior chief so much as uncertainty. But if there was the possibility, however remote, of Traffic's submitting a bill for extra work, it behoved him to inform the superior chief of what was happening before the other gained an incorrect view of events.

He dialled Palma. The plum-voiced secretary told him to wait. He waited.

Salas's manner was as aggressively curt as ever. 'What is it?'

'Inspector Alvarez, señor, from Llueso . . .'

'Good God, man, do you think I don't know where you are based?'

'I have to report that an Englishwoman, Señora Ogden, has disappeared . . .'

'When?'

'She was last seen by her husband on Sunday after lunch . . .'

'It has taken you two days to inform me of the fact?'

'I wanted to be able to make a full and accurate report before I advised you.'

'An admirable ambition, but one that if followed would ensure I never heard from you again.'

'Clearly, it has been essential first to determine whether she disappeared of her own volition or has met some form of trouble. It does seem that her disappearance may be voluntary.'

'On what grounds?'

'Early in the year, she may have been having an affair.'

'It really is extraordinary how keenly you dredge up even the slightest suggestion of salacious behaviour. Have you ever consulted a psychiatrist?'

'Señor, I can only detail the facts as they present themselves.'

'Then present them to me with as few unsavoury details as possible.'

He did so.

'You have learned nothing to confirm the suggestion that the relationship between the señora and Ruffolo is an unnatural one?'

'There's been no suggestion of that.'

'It's only a moment ago you were saying they had committed adultery.'

'Oh! I thought you meant . . .' He came to a stop, certain that it would be a great mistake to explain exactly what he had thought. 'It's true there is no definite proof of an affair, but I did find Señor Ogden's reactions to his wife's failure to return home to be rather unusual. If time were passing and your wife still hadn't turned up, wouldn't you telephone friends to find out if she had stopped off to see them, rather than just getting drunk . . .'

'I am not in the habit of getting drunk,' Salas said angrily.

'Of course not, señor. I was merely trying to explain why his reactions seemed sufficiently unusual to suggest they were significant.'

'What possible significance can there be in a foreigner's becoming drunk? For most of them, that is a natural state.'

'But in his case, I wonder if it points to the fact that he was afraid that she wasn't returning home because she had gone off with another man; that he didn't phone friends because to do so would seem to confirm rumours and expose him to ridicule, whereas if he remained silent it might be that his fears would turn out to be groundless and she'd return. His drinking was to help him hold on to hope and keep his fears at bay.'

'Was the Italian telling the truth when he said he hadn't seen the señora for some time and then only at parties?'

'I'm not certain. I'm sure he's an accomplished liar, but in this instance he may be telling the truth because Señorita Heron would make certain it was very difficult for him to play around.'

'In such a context, the use of the word "play" reveals a deplorable attitude.'

There was a short silence.

'Why was Señor Ogden in hospital?'

'He was suffering from severe food poisoning.'

'But his wife was not?'

'That is so.'

'Did they previously eat in a restaurant and have different dishes or did they eat at home and have different food?'

'I'm afraid I don't know.'

'Why not?'

'I didn't think the question could have any bearing on the señora's disappearance and I . . .'

'An efficient detective is one who understands that until a case is solved it is impossible to be certain what is truly germane and therefore establishes every fact connected with it; a clever detective is one who recognizes that the unexpected, the illogical, the anomaly, the break in routine, the change of character, however apparently inconsequential, perhaps marks the path to the truth. The incompetent detective, on the other hand, is blind to everything but the obvious and is content to accept that without question.'

Alvarez had no doubt into which category he was placed.

'Find out why Señor Ogden suffered food poisoning and Señora Ogden did not.'

'Yes, señor.'

'Have you asked the airlines and ferry companies to check their passenger lists to see if Señora Ogden is known to have left the island?'

'No, señor.'

'Do I have to instruct you in even the most basic steps of an investigation?'

'The trouble is, they always complain so bitterly when we ask them to do something like this. It seemed best to wait until we can be more certain of the señora's probable movements . . .'

'In other words, to pander to their inefficiency is more important than to do your job properly?'

'Of course not . . .'

'Then you will very soon be in a position to tell me whether or not the señora is known to have left the island in the past two days. Do you understand, very soon?'

Since it seemed Salas might be about to ring off abruptly,

Alvarez said hurriedly: 'As I mentioned earlier, Señora Ogden drove off in her car. Its present location could well suggest where she might be.'

'Are you looking for congratulation for having finally shown a spark of constructive thought?'

'Unfortunately, Señor Ogden couldn't remember the registration number and he said there were no papers in the house that would give it. So I asked Traffic to trace the number, using his name and address. It seems this took a long time because their computer is geared to do things the other way round and they're complaining about that and threatening to send us an invoice. But as you've just pointed out, however long the search took, the cost cannot be considered because every fact has to be followed up.'

'How much are they threatening to charge?'

'They haven't said.'

'Did you first repeatedly try to make Señor Ogden remember the number, at times using the proven method of introducing the question suddenly and even violently to jog his memory? Did you order him to search every possible space in his house?'

'I didn't like to trouble him too hard at such an anxious time for him . . .'

'Since when have you considered it right to consider someone's feelings at the department's expense? If Traffic do forward an invoice, I shall personally hold you responsible for meeting it on the grounds of your inability to do your job efficiently.' Salas cut the connection.

Alvarez sighed. He rang central control in Palma and asked them to issue a find-and-report on the missing BMW.

He stepped out of his car and stared at the countryside. Generally, it was poor land; thickly strewn with stones, in many places there were outcrops of rock that made an orderly cultivation impossible; there was very limited underground water so there could be only reduced irrigation; there were small areas where oranges grew, but mostly only fig trees flourished. Yet he coveted this land as much as any other. For a peasant, it was land, of whatever standard, which gave him cause for living and enabled him to endure the harshness of life . . .

There was a shout. 'Have you news?'

He turned to see Ogden hurrying from the house. 'I'm afraid not, señor.'

'Why can't you find her?'

'If she is still on the island, we will.'

'What d'you mean, if she's still on the island? Of course she is. Why d'you say that?'

'Perhaps it would be best if we go inside to talk?' Acting more as host than guest, Alvarez led the way into the cool sitting-room. Once they were both seated, he said: 'Did your wife suffer any symptoms of food poisoning?'

'What's that?'

He repeated the question.

'Sabrina's missing and all you can do is ask if she was ill! God Almighty, I knew you lot were all . . .'

'Señor, it could be important. I assure you that no detail is too small to be overlooked. Was your wife taken ill?'

'No,' Ogden said angrily.

'Did you have a meal at a restaurant on the day you were taken ill?'

'No.'

'You ate at home?'

'If we didn't go out, we stayed at home, didn't we?'

'Did your wife cook something different for herself?'

'No.'

'Then you both ate the same food. So why do you imagine that you suffered serious food poisoning, but the señora did not?' Watching Ogden, Alvarez saw confusion and then panic. Sweet Mary, he thought, the sun had begun to set in the east! Salas was right and the bout of food poisoning was in some way significant.

'I . . . I had more meat than she did,' Ogden mumbled.

'So it was the meat which poisoned you?'

'Yes.'

'Since you were so ill, the meat must have been badly infected. In which case, it seems surprising that your wife did not suffer at least mildly. Can you say why this was?'

'I'm not a doctor.'

'Of course not. But whoever treated you in hospital must have been curious to understand why you were poisoned, but your wife was not – did they not suggest a reason?'

'No.'

'Perhaps not even a doctor can know all the answers . . . Señor, is your wife very friendly with anyone in particular?'

'No.'

'You can suggest no one to whom she might go if extremely troubled, to find the kind of sympathy and understanding that at times a husband is unfortunately unable to offer?'

'What d'you mean?'

Alvarez was puzzled by the other's tone which suddenly was belligerent, yet at the same time seemed to carry a hint of panic. He decided to introduce a small variation of the facts. 'Merely that it sometimes helps to speak to a third party. I've been told she's very friendly with the Keanes.'

'Them? They're no friends of ours.' He paused, then added: 'We used to get on with 'em until he said something to Sabrina that really upset her.'

'What was that?'

'I don't know; I was talking to other people.'

'Didn't she tell you later?'

'She wouldn't, though I kept asking.'

'Why was that?'

'Because she said it was just so stupid, but it would get me really upset and she didn't want that to happen.'

'Then presumably it was something of a very personal nature?'

'I've just said, I don't know.'

'Of course . . . Señor, I am very sorry to have to ask this, but I must. Is it possible your wife has been having an affair?'

Ogden, his features distorted by emotion, shouted a wild, incoherent denial.

Alvarez said goodbye. As he left the sitting-room, he recalled the old saying, 'He who bellows the lie, often whispers the truth.'

As he dipped a finger of coca into the hot chocolate at breakfast on Wednesday morning, Alvarez casually remarked that he would be driving into Palma. Dolores said, 'Oh!' in a manner that invited further comment.

'I have to go to Clinica Afret.'

Her alarm was immediate. 'You are ill? What is wrong? Why have you said nothing?' As were most Mallorquins, she was a hypochondriac, on behalf of her family as well as herself.

'It's nothing to do with me, it's work.'

She relaxed. 'We are having a simple meal today so it won't take long to prepare.'

That was regrettable news. It was only when she complained of the need to spend the entire morning toiling at the stove that one could be certain one would be enjoying the best of her cooking.

She put a cleaned saucepan in the bottom of a cupboard. 'Beatriz rang me only the day before yesterday and said it was so long a time since we'd seen each other.'

Belatedly, he realized the reason for this conversation. 'Why don't you come in with me and I'll drop you off at her place?'

'I've so much to do. No, I don't think so.'

If he accepted her refusal, lunch would be very ordinary indeed. 'You deserve some time off. Let's make it a real holiday for you and when I've finished at the clinic we can have a meal at a restaurant?'

She pulled open a drawer and dropped a couple of kitchen spoons into it. 'I suppose I could ask Elena to feed Isabel and Juan. But she and Jaime don't get on.'

'Then he can stay here and get his own meal. Where's the

problem with that?'

No problem for him.

Beatriz lived in a part of the city not readily accessible from the Ronda and it was a long and frustrating drive through twisting, crowded streets to her house. It was an equally difficult one from there to the clinic which was close to the northern outskirts. When he parked the car, he was hot, thirsty, and ill-tempered.

Haughty indifference to the quality of service provided was not confined to the Spanish bureaucracy; the woman at the information desk listened to his request in sullen silence and then said it was impossible. Even when he identified himself as a detective on active service, it was only with the greatest reluctance that she used the internal phone to call the Accounts Department and tell them that he was asking which doctor had attended Señor Ogden. Her annoyed surprise was obvious when Accounts were able to provide the information without any trouble.

Sequi's surgery was on the second floor of the west wing, the waiting-room on the opposite side of the corridor. As Alvarez sat there, surrounded by people who, he felt certain, were suffering from a variety of serious complaints, he promised himself that from then on he would cut down on his smoking, drinking, and eating, and he would take regular exercise.

The receptionist appeared in the doorway. 'Inspector – the doctor will see you now.'

He left, followed by the resentful stares of those patients who were convinced he had jumped the queue on the strength of his rank. He crossed the corridor into a room that contained several pieces of equipment, all of which carried a sinister air.

'I can give you a couple of minutes, no more,' said the doctor.

Alvarez looked away from a trolley at the end of which were clipped two gas cylinders – for use when a patient had suffered a crippling heart attack? . . . 'I'll be as quick as I can. I understand you treated Señor Ogden when he was here recently?'

'That's correct.'

'He told me that he was suffering from very severe food poisoning as a result of eating infected meat. Is that the full story?'

'Why d'you want to know?'

'Señor Ogden's wife has disappeared and I'm trying to discover whether she left home voluntarily or something drastic has happened to her.'

'And precisely how will knowing the cause of his illness help you decide that?'

'To tell the truth, I'm not certain it will. But in every case, I try to establish all the details, even if on the face of things they don't seem to be relevant, because quite often doing this reveals a hitherto unsuspected important fact,' said Alvarez glibly, paraphrasing Salas's words. 'Both he and his wife ate the meal which poisoned him, so it seems rather odd to a layman that even though he had more meat than she did, she didn't suffer any degree of poisoning.'

'The causative agent was not meat, or any other food for that matter.'

'Then what was it?'

'Cantharidin poisoning. The first case I've come across in twenty years.'

'What exactly is that?'

'The active principle of cantharides, which is the crushed bodies of beetles called . . .' He swung his swivelling chair around until he could reach across and open the right-hand door of a glass-fronted bookcase. He brought out a book, put it on his desk and opened it. *Cantharis vesicatoria*. I should have remembered, since it's used as a vesicatory plaster.'

'What kind of plaster?'

'It raises blisters on the skin to treat inflammations by causing the body to take defensive measures.'

'How on earth did the señor come to eat something like that?'

'Cantharides has a second identity – Spanish fly.'

'The aphrodisiac?' Alvarez said, surprise raising his voice.

'The so-called aphrodisiac. Further, it is not a fly, but a beetle, and is not peculiar to Spain but is found in many other countries. The name is an example of how some nationalities will stoop to any lengths to hide their own iniquities.'

'Señor Ogden had been using that stuff?'

'On his arrival, we had no idea what was the problem. He was suffering burning pains in the mouth, along the oesophagus, in the pit of the stomach and the remainder of the abdomen. He claimed he'd eaten something that was poisoning him and we tried, and failed, to identify what that could be. Further symptoms developed which made it clear that the poisoning was of a most unusual kind, but we made no progress until, in fear of death, he finally admitted he had taken cantharides. This enabled us to treat the symptoms, which we did with considerable success. He probably is too stupid to realize how fortunate he is not only to survive, but to do so suffering such little permanent damage.'

'Why on earth did he take it?'

'That is not obvious?'

'Yes, of course,' Alvarez answered, in some confusion. 'What I meant was, why risk something so dangerous?'

'I talked to his wife, who did not suffer the embarrassed reluctance to tell the truth which so nearly cost him his life, and she explained that there had been difficulties for some time. She tried to persuade him to seek medical advice, but he refused to do so. Inevitably, the situation deteriorated until in desperation he decided on a dangerous attempt to resolve the problem and bought some cantharides.

'Learning about the purchase, she tried to persuade him not to take such a risk; when he insisted on doing so, she took the precaution of researching the subject as far as possible and learned that the fatal dose of the beetle substance is generally held to be between two and three grams; she warned him never to take anything approaching that amount.' The doctor sat back, folded his arms across his chest. 'Ironically, although medically speaking the substance is useless as an aphrodisiac, in his case it proved to be reasonably effective; belief can be the strongest of medicines.'

'If he knew how much was dangerous, how come he overdosed?'

'He maintained he never did. However, his wife told me

that recently he has been drinking heavily and so it seems reasonable to accept that through inebriated carelessness, he made a serious mistake.' He unfolded his arms.

'What impression did you gain about their relationship?'

'The marriage was clearly under very considerable strain and from some of the facts I learned from her, one could not have criticized her had she left him. That she stayed with him, helping him as far as she could, suggests a very strong sense of loyalty. One hopes he has enough sense to appreciate that.'

Alvarez thanked the doctor and left. He wondered if Ogden was as convinced of his wife's loyalty?

Alvarez opened the bottom right-hand drawer of his desk and brought out a bottle of Soberano and a glass. He poured out a very generous amount of brandy. There were times when Dutch courage was essential.

He dialled Palma.

'Superior Chief Salas's office,' said the plum-voiced secretary, as if announcing royalty.

'Inspector Alvarez here. Can I have a word with him?'

As he waited, he drained the glass.

'Has the woman turned up?' Salas demanded.

'No, señor.'

'Have you found out if she left the island?'

'I'm still waiting to hear from both the airline companies and the ferry people.'

'Has the car been found?'

'Not yet.'

'Why not? Why does everything on this island take twice as long as anywhere else?'

Alvarez wondered why Madrileños were always in such a rush when the only effect of this was that they were for ever tripping up over their own feet? 'Señor, I have visited the clinic where Señor Ogden was treated and have spoken to the doctor concerned. Although Señor Ogden told me he was poisoned by meat, this was not true, so that the fact he had eaten more than his wife was of no account . . .'

'If it was of no account, there's no need to waste my time mentioning the fact.'

'He was poisoned by cantharides.'

'What's that?'

'Crushed beetle. And this isn't restricted to Spain, despite the name it's commonly known by . . .'

'Are you capable of reporting anything other than inconsequential negatives?'

'The crushed beetle is often called Spanish fly.'

'Possibly an entomologist would find that fact of interest. I do not.'

'The name doesn't mean anything to you?'

'It does not.'

'Well, it's . . .' His courage temporarily failed him. 'It's used to produce blisters on the skin. But it does have a secondary role.'

'As what?'

'It's not strictly speaking a medical one . . .'

'Goddamnit, man, can you never stop enumerating negatives?'

Alvarez took a deep breath. 'It's popularly, but apparently incorrectly, known as an aphrodisiac.'

'My God! You really do rejoice in wallowing in the iniquities of mankind!'

Alvarez leaned forward and poured himself a second, and larger, drink.

CHAPTER 10

On Thursday morning, the main ferry company operating from the island rang Alvarez to say that since Sunday no Señora Ogden had been listed as a passenger. Within the next hour, three of the airlines reported that she was not on any of their lists. At twenty-five past one, as he was about to leave for home, the phone rang yet again.

'With reference to the green BMW on which there's a search-and-report. One of our units was called to the airport to sort out some bother and they saw the BMW in the car park. It's locked and the only thing visible is a bit of crumpled-up paper in the front passenger well. What d'you want done about it?'

Little could be lost by delaying any search of the car, whilst much might be gained, since something Dolores had said earlier had suggested that she was preparing Bacalao a la Vizcaína for lunch. 'I'll drive in this afternoon after I've finished some very pressing work in hand. Can you have someone meet me there at five-thirty with a set of keys?'

'Will do.' After giving reference figures for the parking spot, the caller rang off.

Alvarez stared at the telephone. That the car had been left at the airport very strongly suggested that Sabrina had left the island by air. Then she had flown in a plane of one of the companies which had not yet reported in, she had flown under a false name – difficult if tickets were matched with passports at the check-in, but this only happened when someone could be bothered – or she had flown on a ticket issued to someone else and the seller had agreed to do the checking-in. Why would she have left the island without a word to her husband? Had the problems of the marriage and then his serious illness put her under such a strain that she had had to escape? Had she formed a relationship with another man so intense that it ruled her brain as well as her heart? Who was the lover? It was not Ruffolo, unless she had left on her own and he would be joining her later. Had she flown to the logical destination – Britain? . . . The questions seemed endless, but for once that was of small account. Since it seemed so logical to assume she had left the island voluntarily, the problem of her present whereabouts no longer concerned him. A satisfactory conclusion.

He left his office and went down and out to his car in the old square. He had forgotten to put on top of the dashboard an indication of when he'd parked, and under the windscreen-wiper blade was a ticket. He crumpled it up and dropped it on to the road. In the past, any member of the Policia Local would have recognized his car and not made a fool of himself by issuing a ticket. Efficiency was progress. Like hell it was!

It was small wonder that the BMW had been identified by chance rather than design – it was one of hundreds of cars which filled the parking area to overflowing. Alvarez walked round the car, then said to the cabo: 'Can you open it now?'

'I hope so, but this marque can be real sods!' The cabo went over to the police Renault, parked without regard to the flow of traffic between the rows of cars, and collected from it several bunches of keys. Contrary to his prior pessimism, he succeeded in unlocking the driving door in a surprisingly short time.

'Obviously your métier!' Alvarez said.

'Watch me after I retire. In a couple of years I'll be so rich, even the Director-General salutes me.'

Alvarez opened the doors in turn, visually searching each inside area. That done, he picked up the crumpled piece of paper in the front passenger well and smoothed it out between his fingers. It was a receipt from the Supermarket Viranyo in Inca; it listed one item at nine thousand seven hundred pesetas and was dated the seventh. He put it in his hip pocket.

He found nothing else of the slightest consequence. 'You

can lock up again. I'll let the husband know it's here and he can collect it – always provided he finds the spare key.'

'If he doesn't, give him my name. I'll only charge him fifteen thousand ... How come the husband didn't know where his wife's car was?'

'She left home Sunday afternoon and that's the last he saw of her.'

'Sounds as if she's a foreigner?'

'English.'

'Never know where you are with them, do you?'

'No, you don't,' Alvarez replied with considerable feeling.

The drive was an easy one, thanks to the via de centura and the autoroute, and in less than half an hour, he turned into the car park of Supermarket Viranyo, on the outskirts of Inca. Once inside the store, he spoke to one of the women at the checkouts and she directed him to the offices to the rear of the building.

The manager was young, sharp and aggressively efficient and, while he did not challenge Alvarez's right to make inquiries, his manner made it rather too clear that he doubted the ability. 'It's straightforward,' he said, as he looked up from the receipt.

'Maybe to you, but not to me,' Alvarez replied. 'What was bought?'

'A bottle of scent.'

'You sell that sort of stuff?'

'Several months ago, I suggested to the board in my monthly report that a small section of shelving should be devoted to ladies' luxury toiletries. They were doubtful at first – they're far too conservative – but I was quite right. Sales have been excellent and shelf profits higher.'

The manager did not doubt his own brilliance. 'What kind of scent was it?'

'I would have to check against the stocklists.'

'Would you do that? And can you identify who was at the till?'

'Of course.'

'I'd like a word with her.'

'Why?'

'To ask her if she can remember who bought the perfume.'

'Are you serious? With the business we do, that's impossible. Sheer waste of time.'

'Nevertheless, I'd like to ask her.'

'It'll be very inconvenient.'

'I'm sure you'll be able to arrange matters,' Alvarez said smoothly.

The manager, his expression one of annoyance, left. Alvarez stared at the large photograph of the head and shoulders of a man in a very ornate, golden frame, which hung on the wall opposite the desk. There was a nameplate and, curious to see who was so honoured, he crossed the floor to read this. Antonio Viranyo, founder of Viranyo S.A. He wondered why the successful and rich so often looked as if they were constipated.

The manager returned and sat before saying: 'The name of the scent is Feux d'Amour.'

'Sounds like hot stuff!'

He was not amused.

'Have you found out who sold it?'

'Ana Ortiz, who is working at number three checkout. I have asked her to close her till and come here as soon as she can. I trust you will take up as little of her time as possible.'

Alvarez tried to make conversation, but the manager was so clearly uninterested in anything he had to say that he soon retired into silence. On the island, the gulf between the young and their elders was wider and deeper than in most places. The young had always known the world beyond the borders of Spain, their elders had not, and this fact was reflected in outlook and the appreciation and resentment of both the pleasures and the pains of life . . .

A woman, in her late teens, wearing a pinafore with the company's logo printed over her dress, came into the office.

'He's from the Cuerpo General de Policia,' said the manager, much as if introducing someone caught shoplifting.

She faced Alvarez. 'Is something wrong?' she asked challengingly, yet also defensively.

'Nothing, señorita,' he answered with a smile. 'I merely need to ask if you can remember who bought a bottle of scent called Feux d'Amour on Monday.'

She shook her head. 'There's no way.'

'But I don't suppose you sell a lot of bottles which cost nine thousand seven hundred pesetas?'

'You'd be surprised!'

'I have tried to explain to the inspector how successful the new toiletry section has been,' said the manager.

'Do you think you sold more than one bottle of that scent on Monday?' Alvarez asked.

She hesitated. 'I don't know,' she finally replied.

'The purchase doesn't stick in your mind since it was just the one, expensive item?'

The question perplexed her.

'Surely most people buy lots of things in a supermarket, not just one?'

'Not always. We get 'em in for just a loaf of bread because it's cooked three times a day.'

He accepted that she could remember nothing about the purchaser. 'Thank you, señorita.'

As she left the office, the manager said: 'Is that all?'

'Everything,' Alvarez replied, 'except to thank you for your willing help.'

He returned to his car, but did not immediately drive off. The facts now suggested that Sabrina had spent Sunday night somewhere to the east of Inca; on Monday, she had set off to drive to the airport; en route, she had decided to stop at the supermarket to buy a bottle of scent. To a male mind, it seemed odd that having geared up her mind to fleeing her husband, she should break the journey for so trivial a reason, but to a female mind, perhaps it was perfectly logical . . .

He started the engine and drove out of the car park on to the road.

As Ogden stood in the doorway of his house, he said wildly: 'Why haven't you found her?'

'Señor,' Alvarez replied quietly, 'I am here now because I have learned certain facts which I need to discuss with you.'

65

'What?'

'I think it would be best if we went inside.'

Ogden hesitated, then stepped back. He led the way through to the patio. On the table was a bottle of whisky, a soda syphon, an ice container, and a glass; he picked up the glass and drained it. About to pour himself another drink, he checked his movements. 'I suppose you want something?'

'I would certainly enjoy a small coñac.'

Ogden returned into the house. Alvarez sat on one of the chairs set around the table. This was his favourite time of the day – the world had stilled, the cloudless sky had become tinged with violet to mark approaching darkness, and the temperature was almost bearable. Sounds were travelling long distances, yet for once there was not a single dog which broke the peace with its aimless barking. By listening carefully, he could just catch the distant clanging of bells that marked a herd of sheep on the move, searching for anything edible in fields scorched brown . . .

Ogden returned, put a glass down on the table in front of Alvarez, sat. 'Shall I tell you something,' he said with renewed belligerence. 'I don't think you're really trying to find her.'

'Señor, I am here because I have been making many inquiries and I need to know whether the señora uses scent?'

'Does what? Jesus! You try to make out you're doing something and then ask that?'

'The answer may be very important.'

'How?'

'You will soon understand. Does she use scent?'

'Of course she does.'

'Has she a favourite brand?'

'You expect me to know that when I'm living a nightmare, thinking of her lying somewhere, slowly dying.'

'I don't think you need fear such a tragedy.'

'You don't? You've no idea where she is or what has happened to her, yet you sit there and give me smug assurances that aren't worth a bloody farthing.'

'Please try and answer me.'

'I don't know and I don't give a damn.'

'Might there be a bottle of scent in the bathroom or bedroom that would tell you the kind she liked?'

'And do you want to know what make of shoes she wears? And does she brush her teeth up and down or side to side?'

'Just the kind of scent.'

Ogden drank heavily, put the glass down, stood, held on to the table for a moment to secure his balance, then walked carefully into the house.

Ogden's manner seemed to be touched with something close to hysteria, Alvarez thought. Alcohol induced, or was there some strong emotion which had to be hidden gripping him?

Ogden returned, slumped down on his chair.

'Have you found a bottle of your wife's scent?'

'I told her, the stuff's nothing more than alcohol and a bit of synthetic stink. Fifty quid for enough to dampen the back of your hand! If you want to be a millionaire, start making scent and give it a bloody silly Frog name.' He drank.

'What is the name?'

'Feux . . . Feux . . .' The third time, he succeeded in saying: 'Feux d'Amour.'

'Then I can tell you, señor, that almost certainly the señora spent Sunday night not far from here and on Monday she drove to the airport, stopping off at a supermarket in Inca on the way. As yet I do not have confirmation that she flew from the island on Monday, but I think we can be certain that she did.'

'Impossible!'

'Her car is at the airport and in it is a receipt from the Supermarket Viranyo in Inca for the purchase which was made on Monday of a small bottle of Feux d'Amour.'

Ogden was silent for several seconds, then he shouted: 'Why should she do that?'

'You can answer that question more readily than I.'

'What d'you mean?'

'Only you can be certain if she had reason to leave you.'

'Of course she bloody didn't.'

'Two days ago, I went to Clinica Afret and spoke to Dr Sequi.

You were not poisoned by bad meat, but by an overdose of a substance that is commonly called Spanish fly.'

Ogden made a sound at the back of his throat that was not a cry, yet contained the pain of one. Alvarez looked away and at the hills, sadly certain that little could be more humiliating than having one's private self exposed.

'The doctor shouldn't have told you; it's a breach of professional confidence; I'll have him struck off the register.'

'Since the information may be very germane to my investigation into your wife's disappearance, it was his duty to give it to me.'

'It's nothing to do with it. I suppose you're laughing at me like all those bastards did in the hospital?'

'Señor, I have learned never to laugh at anyone for fear they can all too easily find cause to laugh at me. Life had become very difficult for both of you, hadn't it?'

'No.'

'And when you were so ill, the señora was put under even greater strain emotionally. Isn't it very possible that when she could be certain you would fully recover, she felt she had to leave here to be on her own for a while?'

'No.'

'Then has she formed a friendship, perhaps with a younger man, that she has decided to pursue?'

'She loves me,' Ogden shouted wildly. 'D'you hear, she loves me. You're a fool to think she'd ever leave me for anyone else.'

'Whatever the cause of her leaving the island, I have to assume that she did so voluntarily. This means the case is no longer a police matter and I am closing the investigation.'

'I've always known this place is still in the Dark Ages, but this is bloody ridiculous! She's not gone anywhere voluntarily. She's in trouble. You've got to find her . . .'

'Her car is at the airport and I've written down the reference number of the parking spot.' Alvarez brought a square of paper out of the pocket of his shirt and put that down on the table. 'It's locked, so you'll need to take the spare key; if you haven't one, ask the local BMW agents to help.

There's no sign of the ticket so you'll need to explain the circumstances to the attendant at the gates.' He stood.

'Why won't you understand? Because I'm a foreigner? What the hell does it matter to you that I'm going crazy with worry?'

'As I have just explained . . .'

'You've explained bloody nothing.'

Alvarez turned towards the door of the house.

Ogden's tone changed. 'For God's sake, I beg you, help me.'

Alvarez was scornful of this change from angry rudeness to humble supplication, yet knew sympathy for the other – what could be more emotionally traumatic than fearing one's wife had gone off with another man while grasping at the faint hope that she had not? 'There is only one thing more I can do. If you will give me the names and addresses of your wife's friends in England, I will ask the authorities there to find out if any of them can say where she is now.'

After merienda at the Club Llueso, Alvarez returned to the post and settled behind his desk. Saturday! Lacking any major incident, work would stop at lunchtime and not resume until Monday morning. However, there was one cloud on the horizon. It was necessary to phone Salas . . . If the devil beckoned, it was pointless trying to run away. He reached forward and picked up the receiver, dialled.

'Superior Chief Salas's office.'

'Inspector Alvarez speaking, señorita. May I have a word with the superior chief?'

'He is not here this morning. He has very important duties elsewhere.'

The cloud disappeared as he remembered reading in the *Diario de Mallorca* that an amateur golf tournament was starting that day. 'Then may I leave a message? I have good reason to believe Señora Ogden has flown to the United Kingdom of her own accord, despite the lack of confirmation through the airline companies, and this means we are no longer concerned with her disappearance; however, in order that Señor Ogden may be satisfied we are doing everything in our power – as the superior chief has so pertinently pointed out, good public relations are essential in all dealings with foreigners – I suggest it would be a good idea to ask the English authorities to check with the friends whose names the señor has supplied to find out whether any of them has news of her present whereabouts.'

'Is that all?'

'Yes, señorita.'

She cut the connection with the same rude abruptness that Salas would have shown.

After replacing the receiver, he studied the clutter on his

desk. With nothing urgent in hand, this was obviously the time to find out if any of the unopened mail was important and to sort and tidy all the papers and files . . . But it was very hot and man was not made to work in excessive heat . . .

He awoke in time to hurry home to lunch.

On Thursday, he was contemplating nothing in particular when the internal phone buzzed. 'There's a man here wants to see you,' said the duty cabo.

'About what?'

'How would I know?'

'Perhaps by asking him?'

'He's English and speaks Spanish like a dying duck, so you can have that pleasure.'

This surely meant trouble in one form or another; most of the island's problems were caused by foreigners. Reluctantly, he came to his feet and made his way downstairs.

Standing by the desk of the duty cabo was a tall, well-built man who wore a suit. Such unusual elegance worried Alvarez. He said in English, his tone wary: 'Good morning, señor. I am Inspector Alvarez.'

'Aubrey Maitland.' He shook hands briskly. 'It's been quite a job tracking you down – no one seemed to know where to find you.'

'I suppose the problem was that members of the Cuerpo generally operate from the quarters of the Policia Armada y de Trafico, but Llueso is an exception.' An exception designated temporary; in Spanish, 'temporary' had many meanings.

'At least it provided the taxi driver with a profitable fare.' He smiled.

Maitland's manner was warm and friendly and Alvarez smiled back, despite his worry that this meeting might disrupt his morning's schedule.

'I'm here hoping to discuss someone of interest to both of us – Bevis Ogden.'

'Then perhaps you would like to come up to my office?'

'May I suggest an alternative? That we combine pleasure with business and find a restaurant where we can have a chat

71

over a drink, or two, and a good meal. Would that suit you and if so, can you recommend somewhere?'

'It's very kind of you, but first I must check if I've any work too urgent to be delayed.'

'Of course.'

Alvarez spoke to the cabo. 'Find the señor a chair.'

Scowling, the cabo stood and made his way towards the far doorway beyond the stairs.

Switching back to English, Alvarez said: 'I will not be long. I have told the cabo to bring you a chair so that you can sit while you wait.'

'Thanks, but you needn't have bothered. It's good to stand.'

The English suffered many peculiarities. Alvarez made his way to his office, sat, mopped the sweat from his forehead and neck, picked up the receiver and dialled. When Dolores answered the call, he said, sounding suitably rushed: 'Some very urgent work has just come in which means I may not be able to get away on time. Will that upset lunch?'

'Why should it?'

'You might be preparing something special.'

'I had to help Luisa who's been ill and whose no-good husband thinks the best way of getting her better is to spend his day drinking in a café, so I've only just returned home. It will have to be a very small lunch.'

'Then it won't matter too much if I do have to stay on here, working?'

'What will you do for a meal?'

'Perhaps I'll nip out for some tapas.'

'You shouldn't let them mess you around like this.'

'Sometimes one has to sacrifice oneself for the good of the community.'

'I'll see there's a good supper to make up for it.'

Truly, one could have one's cake and eat it. 'No man deserves such kindness.'

'That's true. But I am a fool who does not stop to think the truth.'

He replaced the receiver. He was being asked to choose the restaurant. Since the size of the bill would not concern him, quality, not quantity, was the criterion. But to find quality was not all that easy because a restaurant which served a memorable meal yesterday might well provide a forgettable one today – Mallorquin chefs were notably men of moods. That remembered, people were praising the Montserrat which had a French chef which should mean greater consistency. The Annera amb naps was reputedly of unsurpassable quality . . .

Beyond the converted finca there was a wide patio, shaded overhead by mats of split bamboo, and a large swimming pool; the boundary of the property was marked by a row of vines, trained on wires, and a stone wall.

'This,' said Maitland, who had removed coat and tie, 'is heaven! Doubly so since it was overcast and drizzling at Gatwick.'

The scene was made even more attractive by the two young ladies who, topless, were sunbathing on the far side of the pool.

A waiter came up to their table and put on it two glasses, each containing several cubes of ice, poured brandy into one and gin into the other. He left a bottle of tonic by the side of the glass, hurried off.

Maitland studied his glass. 'If a publican gave one this much gin at home, one would know he'd flipped!' He added tonic, then raised his glass. 'To an island that's learned the art of living.' He drank. 'What about getting the business over with so we can enjoy our meal in peace?' he suggested as he put his glass down.

'A very good idea.' The other might be English, Alvarez thought, but his instincts were civilized.

'I'll begin with a little history. For several years I worked in the insurance world as a loss adjuster, and modesty should, but doesn't, prevent me saying I was quite good at the job; sufficiently active, anyway, to come to the notice of several companies after becoming something of a thorn in their sides. So presumably it was on the principle of poacher turning gamekeeper that I was approached to join a newly constituted organization.

'For years, insurance companies suffered an increasing number of suspect claims which had been carried out with sufficient skill to make the proving of fraud very, very difficult. As time went on, it became clear that when a fraud was successful against one company, it would be repeated against another, but because of professional embarrassment at being made a sucker, there was no exchange of information between the first and the second, so the latter was not forewarned by the preliminary moves; worse, afterwards, all the available evidence of both cases would not be viewed together when to do that might well provide the necessary proof.

'A few heads were banged together until they stopped wittering on about the perils of sharing confidential information and then the majority of companies agreed to set up a special investigative umbrella body to which all known or suspected fraudulent claims, or even those that didn't smell right, would be referred so that details could be compared with other cases and any apparent similarities noted, whereupon a very detailed and extensive investigation would be carried out . . . Which brings me to Bevis Ogden. Has his wife reappeared?'

'No. Despite the fact that no airline reports carrying someone of her name on any flight after Sunday, the sixth, the evidence suggests she flew back to Britain on or after the Monday. Following up this probability, I've asked for inquiries to be made in England among her friends.'

'Which, in a slightly roundabout way, is why I'm here now . . . For many years, Ogden had his life insured for half a million pounds and his wife's – Dorothy – for a quarter of a million. On their divorce, he immediately cancelled her policy. On his marriage to Belinda, he took out a policy on her life for half a million. For three years, premiums were paid, then Ogden informed the company that he had just learned his wife had died and he would be claiming on the policy as sole beneficiary of her estate. Asked for the death certificate, he said that he'd already been in touch with Spain, where she had died, and requested it be sent to him . . . To register a claim even before obtaining the death certificate suggests unusual urgency, so it'll be no surprise to know that it was viewed with – as they say – a measure of suspicion. After making certain inquiries, the insurance company concerned passed the file over to us with a request for a full investigation . . . How much do you know about Ogden's background?'

'Almost nothing.'

'Then I'll paint in the essentials so you can understand the course of our inquiry and I'll list them as finally assembled, not in the chronological order in which we uncovered them.' Maitland drained his glass. 'Talking is thirsty work. You'll join me in another?'

'Thank you.'

He signalled to a waiter who came across, took the order, carried off the dirty glasses.

'Ogden,' Maitland said, 'worked as a commodity broker. He married Dorothy thirty-five years ago. She has been described as warm hearted and generous, but not the kind of woman to make heads turn. He earned a very considerable salary and in addition invested heavily in Lloyd's.

'Roughly eight years ago, he met Belinda. Much younger than he; to judge from photographs she'd make most male heads turn so sharply there'd be a lot of ricked necks.' The waiter returned and put two glasses and a full bottle of tonic on the table. Maitland filled his glass. 'From all accounts, he conceived such a grand passion for Belinda that he made a laughing stock of himself. However, Dorothy didn't have that kind of a sense of humour and after trying to make him see sense, and failing, she divorced him.

'He married Belinda almost before the ink was dry on the divorce papers. He'd had to make a large settlement on Dorothy, but was still a reasonably wealthy man and Belinda was able to spend, spend, spend.

'When Lloyd's first met big trouble, he appeared to be all right because none of the syndicates he was with seemed to have been involved in the areas of huge losses. But then it turned out that one of them had been, but had fraudulently been concealing the fact. As a result, all the names were called on to make heavy payments and, as one of the bigger investors, his debts were considerable.

'He could have retrenched – met his debts by liquidating assets, moving into a smaller house, leading a more frugal life. But with a much younger wife who, he must have realized in his saner moments, had married him for his money, that option wasn't open to him because if their lifestyle became too reduced, she'd be off. So they continued to lead an unfettered life of luxury with the inevitable result that soon he was facing financial meltdown.

'The firm in the City for which he worked had an absolute rule that no partner should trade on his own behalf. Desperate to find money from somewhere, Ogden began trading for himself. This fact was discovered and he was sacked. So now he was without a job, very low on capital, and married to a young woman who was not going to welcome a life of hardship. Before long, he owed money everywhere, his bank was for ever writing him nasty letters, credit cards were withdrawn, friends started having previous engagements . . . All the usual problems of growing poor with an additional one – either he found a fresh source of money or he was going to lose Belinda.

'One day, she did not return home after shopping. Late that night, he contacted the police. As usual, initially they did not give the case priority since there were no circumstances suggesting criminal activity and most missing persons soon reappear. But she didn't. And after a while, they judged the case to be serious and stepped up their investigation.

'Ten days after her disappearance, Ogden received a letter, posted in Paris, in which Belinda wrote that she'd left him because she'd met someone else. He showed this letter to the police, which brought the investigation to an abrupt stop.

'Four months later, he received a letter, signed Jim – no surname – which told him that after suffering very serious injury following a fall, Belinda had died; before she'd died, she'd managed to write the note which he enclosed. This was a rambling, mawkish attempt to justify her desertion.

'Immediately after receiving this news of her death, he claimed under her life policy which, as I said, triggered inquiries. One of the first things to interest us was the fact that when Dorothy divorced him, he cancelled her policy immediately, yet when Belinda left him for another man, he did not cancel hers. We asked him why he had let Belinda's run on when he found it so difficult to keep up premium payments and his answer was that he'd been hoping against hope she'd return to him. It really is true that there's no fool like an old fool in love, but he was in deep financial trouble and his wife was insured for a large sum and that's a classic recipe for fraud.

'Eventually, he gave us the death certificate. Naturally, we asked the Spanish authorities to validate this and after a long while, and at considerable expense, they did. Which obviously brought to an end all suspicions and the half million was paid out. One cynic said that Ogden would never realize how lucky he was to be able to exchange an aging debt for a growing asset.

'Time moved on. Then, a couple of days ago, I was phoned by a detective with whom we'd had some contact when investigating the claim on Belinda. He thought I'd be interested to know that Sabrina, third wife of Bevis Ogden, had disappeared from her home in Mallorca and he had been asked to try and find out if any of her old friends in England had news of her whereabouts. To have one wife disappear is a misfortune; to have a second one do likewise seems a coincidence too far. I immediately contacted all insurance companies and asked if any of them had written a life policy on Sabrina Ogden. The answer was that eighteen months previously, one of them had, through its Spanish branch, for half a million sterling . . . That news had me booking the first possible flight out here.'

Alvarez said slowly: 'The successful criminal so often makes the mistake of trying to repeat his success.'

'Luckily for the law! Presumably, the Ogdens have been leading a very expensive life?'

'I would imagine so, from the little I've seen.'

'Even though half a million is a fortune to the average person, for a big spender it can soon need topping up . . . In Sabrina's proposal form, she gave her age as twenty-five and four months which means she's closing on twenty-seven now. Had she lived, Belinda Ogden would be almost twenty-seven. Did you meet Sabrina before she disappeared?'

'No. But Señor Ogden gave me a recent snap of her to help me in my inquiries.'

Maitland had hung his coat on the back of the chair and he turned and brought out of the inside pocket a leather wallet; from this, he produced a photograph which he handed across. 'Mrs Belinda Ogden.'

Alvarez studied the woman who stood poised as if about to break into a run. Sensuously attractive, few men would look at her without secret thoughts. In his mind, he compared her with the woman in the photograph – back at the post – which Ogden had given him. Belinda looked different, in slight, subtle ways. But a trained observer knew to concentrate on those features which could not be altered by mere style, and he had noted, with no specific reason for doing so at the time, the way in which Sabrina's ears were set higher than normal and possessed what was called a Darwinian tubercle, a slight bump on the outside at the top. Belinda's ears were similarly positioned and shaped. 'I think the two women are the same.'

'Then we can fill in some of the details. Belinda went to Paris and, to the prearranged plan, sent him the letter. Later, she moved to Spain and arranged for a false death certificate. Ogden claimed on her insurance policy and once the money was paid, left England, no doubt saying the country held too many bitter memories for him. They met up again and moved to this island. He'd carefully told none of his friends where they were living, but as there had to be the hundred to one chance that they'd eventually run into someone they knew, she changed her appearance as far as that was reasonably possible so that she could just shrug her shoulders and say that everyone has a lookalike somewhere.

'Once settled here, she continued to demand a life of expensive luxury. Ogden realized that if things continued as they were going, it wouldn't be all that long before money once more became a real problem, yet even then he couldn't bring himself to try to curb her spending and sought another way of solving the problem.

'He decided to work the insurance scam for a second time. He took out a policy on her life with a different company from the previous one, waited for as long as he reckoned was essential, then arranged her disappearance.

'By analogy, the future's predictable. He'll receive a letter to say she's with another man, which is a clever move because the new relationship means that he will have no apparent contact with her and no control over her actions. Then, after a month or two, there'll be a note from Dick, Dave, or Ted, to say she's died in an accident. A death certificate will still any doubts there might be . . . Does that sound feasible?'

'Very much so.'

'Of course, there is something which on the face of things makes nonsense of everything I've said. The Spanish authorities validated Belinda's death certificate . . .' He became silent.

'You are wondering if there has been corruption?'

'And as a visitor, that is a very insulting thing to do.'

'To some extent, your job is like mine – it continually calls on us to insult by suspicion,' Alvarez said sadly. 'If Belinda and Sabrina are the same person, then of course the death certificate was obtained by corruption. It has to be the doctor and probably the undertaker as well, since they are directly involved; but probably not the bureaucrats since they merely accept the facts they're given and then legalize them by recording them.'

'Sadly, in every profession in every country there is always someone ready to let the side down,' Maitland said, trying to lessen the sense of resentful shame Alvarez might be feeling. He drank most of what was left in his glass. 'Ogden's plan must be to leave the island once the money's paid and to join her in another part of the world. Possibly, even now he's thinking about the chance of a third fraud, convinced he's hit on the perfect way to make a living.'

'There is perhaps an ironic twist to events this time.'

'In what way?'

'Before you told me all this, I judged he was scared she really *had* gone off with another man.'

'That could be her undeclared price for taking part in the fraud and he's had to accept the fact, even while trying to deny it to himself. Maybe there really was a Jim. Maybe there have been lots of Jims because Ogden can only provide her with money, not excitement.'

79

'I might have been mistaken about his feelings. Perhaps he is a good actor and knew that if he could make me think she was betraying him, my sympathy would make me less likely to doubt all he told me . . . We must speak to him.'

'As soon as we've finished lunch?'

'I have to return to the office to do some work. Shall I pick you up at six at your hotel?'

'Fine. That'll give me the time for a good swim.'

A swim in preference to a siesta?

CHAPTER 12

As they turned off the road on to the short dirt track down to Ca'n Nou, Maitland said: 'It looks to be quite a house! Has he bought or does he rent?'

'I have no idea,' Alvarez replied as he began to brake.

'What would a place like this cost?'

'Prices have become absurd! There is a house I know which has only three bedrooms and some land and the owner is asking a hundred million pesetas.'

'That's closing on half a million pounds!'

Alvarez brought the car to a halt. 'People have been blinded by pesetas. Prices at this end of the island have always been high because it is the most beautiful, but recently Germans have been paying whatever is asked and now owners demand so much that the mind is confused thinking about it. Even an unreformed finca with no more than a hectare of land and a poor well which dries in the summer is beyond a man's dreams.'

'What goes up, has to come down. The market will crash and you'll be able to go out and buy your dream property.'

'Perhaps I will win El Gordo or the primitive lottery, but I do not think any of the possibilities are very likely.'

As they climbed out of the car, Ogden opened the front door of the house. His face was in shadow, but Alvarez did not miss the sharp change of expression as he recognized Maitland.

'Hullo, there,' Maitland said cheerily as he approached the house, his right hand held out.

Ogden, making no attempt to shake hands, said thickly: 'Why are you here?'

Maitland dropped his hand to his side. 'I thought it would be a good idea to have a chat with you, and Inspector Alvarez kindly brought me along.'

'I've nothing more to say.'

'I'm sure you'll manage to find something.'

'Clear off.'

Alvarez came to a stop. 'May we enter, señor?'

Ogden hesitated, then, without a word, turned and went through the house to the patio where he sat, seemingly careless that his rudeness highlighted his fear.

As Maitland settled on a chair, he said: 'It's interesting that you've not asked if we've news of your wife.'

'The inspector would have told me if he'd finally found the energy to try to find her . . . What the hell d'you want?'

'The answers to a few questions, like do you rent this place or is it yours?'

'That's none of your bloody business. It's nothing to do with what's happened to Sabrina.'

'That is a matter of conjecture. After all, a rented house can be deserted overnight at the loss of only the unused rental period; a house that's owned has to be sold which takes time and the transfer of the purchase price will leave a trail unless one's very smart.'

'Why are you here?'

'That's not obvious? I'm hoping to find out if there's significance in the fact that your third wife has disappeared in similar circumstances to your second.'

'All I know is, she didn't return on the Sunday and I've been living in hell ever since.'

'Because you spend your time wondering if she's enjoying her freedom more fully than your script allows?'

Ogden turned to Alvarez. 'Why aren't you stopping him insulting me?' he shouted.

'I have heard no insults.'

'Then you must be bloody deaf. Or you don't understand English.'

'That is very likely,' Alvarez answered equably. 'Is the señora's passport here, in the house.'

'No.'

'Because she needed it to leave the island?'

'Because she always carries it in her handbag along with all the other papers we have to have with us all the time.'

82

'Would these include her birth and marriage certificates?'

'Yes.'

'She obviously is very concerned to be able to prove who she is.'

'Because of the ridiculous rules in this place.'

Maitland said: 'Where was she born?'

'What business of yours is that.'

'I'll be very interested to know if she was born in Islington. You know why I'll be so interested, don't you?'

Ogden didn't answer.

'Belinda was born in Islington. If we learn Sabrina was likewise, the coincidences really will be piling up. But then I suppose that realistically there's small chance of that. You'll have had the foresight to see she has false papers to avoid the excitement of too much astonishment. Still, who knows what such papers will reveal when they're checked out?'

'You don't give a damn my wife is missing or what it's like for me. All you can do is talk vicious nonsense.'

'Earlier on, the inspector and I had drinks and a meal in delightful surroundings and I showed him a photograph of Belinda. Guess what he said?'

'How the hell can I?'

'It would require very little imagination. He says she looks just like Sabrina.'

'So what?'

'Just one more coincidence?'

'Why d'you think I married Sabrina?'

'Delicacy prohibits an answer.'

'Because she looks so like Belinda.'

'Funnily enough, I said to the inspector that I reckoned that's what you'd probably claim.'

'I suppose you think you're being smart?'

'My headmaster cured me of ever believing that ... Let's be serious. Sabrina and Belinda are one and the same, aren't they?'

'You're crazy.'

'It's quite a clever move for an amateur. But perhaps I wrong you by describing you as an amateur since you used to be a commodity broker, which means you're an expert at buying what you don't wish to receive and selling what you don't possess; a short-sighted pro might be more accurate. Short-sighted because you don't seem to accept that the law usually shows a measure of leniency to someone who realizes he's run his course and admits the truth, thereby saving time and money, rather than trying desperately to delay the inevitable.'

'What truth?'

'It becomes boring to have to spell out everything.'

'Bore me.'

'Back in England you ran so short of money that you and Belinda faked her death in order to claim successfully under her life insurance. You decided to live on this island, satisfied the deception would not come to light. But the money once more started to melt as fast as an icicle in hell and you realized you'd soon need to replenish the coffers. Easy. Your present wife would die in circumstances proven to be profitable. Unfortunately, no one has whispered to you the fact that in the world of crime, success breeds failure. A second wife disappearing with an unknown male, then dying in some foreign field leaving you to claim on a half-million policy? Very difficult to accept.'

'You tried to say Belinda wasn't really dead. So what happened? You had to eat your words!' Ogden said sneeringly. 'I'm not claiming anything because Sabrina's not dead.'

'You admit it?'

'I don't know where she is or what's happened to her, she's not dead.'

'Señor . . .' began Alvarez.

'Get out,' he shouted. 'Clear off.'

Alvarez stood; Maitland did the same. 'After we've gone and you've had time to calm down,' said Maitland, 'think about this. Camouflage is only effective so long as it camouflages. Your stirring declaration of belief in Sabrina's being alive only appears to negate the possibility that you could be attempting to repeat the scam until you make the claim.'

They were halfway to the door of the sitting-room when Alvarez came to a stop. 'Señor, do you and your wife have residencias?'

'No.'

As Alvarez closed the front door behind himself, he said: 'If the señora had a residenctia, we would have her fingerprints. But it should not be difficult to find good prints about this house.'

'What would one compare them with? Back home, people only have their prints taken and held if they're convicted and we've no reason to think Belinda ever was. And the only other verifiable source would be the house she lived in with him, but that's been occupied by other people for too long.' Maitland led the way to the car and settled on the front passenger seat. He said, as he clipped home the seat belt: 'He's admitted nothing, said nothing that takes us an inch forward. We think we know the truth, but can't be certain because improbable coincidences have a nasty habit of turning out to be fact, and reasonable assumptions to be wrong, because life likes to laugh.'

'Which means I must determine whether the death certificate of Belinda is fraudulent. I will make inquiries.'

'I hate to have to ask you to do that.'

'If someone has acted criminally, he must be exposed,' said Alvarez bitterly, knowing that if the death certificate was false, a foreigner, no matter how understanding, would have learnt that Spanish honour had been tarnished.

As Alvarez sat down at the dining-table and reached across for the bottle of brandy, Dolores looked through the bead curtain. 'You are late and I've had to delay supper.'

'I had to make inquiries down in the port.'

'And they, of course, took much longer than you'd expected.' Her tone was both ironic and angry.

'If you're thinking . . .'

'My thoughts are my own.' She withdrew.

'She reckons I've been spending my time with a woman,' Alvarez said to Jaime, as he poured himself a drink.

'Haven't you?'

'No. It was all work.'

'She'll never believe that.'

'Don't I know it.'

'She never believes anything.' He lowered his voice. 'Yet as God is my witness, I never lie to her unless it's absolutely necessary.'

'You're a good husband!'

As Alvarez waited to speak to Salas, receiver to his ear, he watched a gecko scurry a wavy path across the ceiling, then freeze when only a few centimetres out from the wall. When he'd been young, people had been so scared of geckos that on sighting one a woman would scream. Popular myth had said that if a gecko landed on one, the grip of its feet was so great that if one tried to remove it by force, it would rip away the skin. Yet it must have happened relatively frequently that a gecko landed on someone and then frantically scurried off, leaving no physical harm. So how had the myth survived in the face of the truth? How many more beliefs were equally fallacious? . . .

'Yes?' said Salas, his bad temper obvious even over the phone.

'Señor, in connection with the disappearance of Señora Ogden . . .'

'Have you found her?'

'No. But I am convinced she is alive.'

'Then I will assume she is dead.'

'Señor Maitland, from England, who investigates suspected insurance frauds is on the island because . . .' Alvarez briefly detailed the facts. 'So it would seem that the death certificate was false,' he concluded.

'Only if the two women are the same person.'

'If they aren't, the coincidences . . .'

'Have you still not learned that coincidences can never be a substitute for the truth? Have you not stopped to consider the consequence of accepting this Englishman's contention regarding the two señoras?'

'Of course I have, but . . .'

'You find it easy to believe a Spaniard would betray the authority invested in him?'

'It would be very unusual, of course. But it could happen . . .'

'Only in the mind of a Mallorquin.'

'Then I am to make no inquiries into the validity of the death certificate, even though Señor Maitland is convinced it has to be false and no doubt will be telling the British police that?'

There was a long silence. 'There are times,' said Salas bitterly, 'when regretfully one has to humour ignorance.'

'I am to check it out?'

'No doubt you are now about to suggest you should travel to wherever the certificate was issued in order to make inquiries. You will travel nowhere. The inquiries will be made by a local inspector, thus ensuring they are carried out far more quickly and efficiently. Do you have a copy of the certificate?'

'Yes, señor.'

'You will fax it to me right away.' Salas cut the connection.

Alvarez replaced the receiver. He searched amongst the jumble of papers and files on his desk and eventually found the copy of Belinda Ogden's death certificate which Maitland had given him the previous day. She had died in Las Macaulas from multiple injuries following a fall at Son Jordi; the doctor's signature was an indecipherable scrawl. Son Jordi was in the Pyrenees, some thirty kilometres inland, and the trip would have provided a pleasant break . . .

He climbed out of his car and the sounds of splashing water made him, as absurd as this might be, feel cooler. He crossed to the front door of Ca Na Ada and rang the bell.

The door was opened by a middle-aged woman in maid's uniform. 'Is Señor Ruffolo in?' he asked.

'No, he's not.'

There was a call. 'Who is it, Marta?'

She turned and spoke to the open doorway of the sitting-room in fractured English to say she didn't know.

Alvarez had recognized the voice. 'Señorita Heron, it is me.'

'And who the hell's me?' Ada, as inappropriately dressed as ever, stepped into the hall. 'So me's you. After more booze?'

About to deny the insulting suggestion, he checked the words, convinced that an earnest denial on his part would merely provoke her contempt. 'Provided it's from a good bodega.'

She laughed. 'You're an insolent bastard! . . . Marta, champagne, brandy, and ice.'

He followed her through the sitting-room to the pool complex. She slumped down on the swing chair which had been set up since he was last there. 'If it gets any hotter, I'll dissolve.'

He wondered why she didn't remain indoors and enjoy the air conditioning? The English seemed afraid of comfort. Perhaps they believed discomfort fortified the soul.

'So what do you want?' she demanded.

'I wish to speak to Señor Ruffolo.'

'Do you now? Why?'

'To ask him some questions.'

Marta, a tray in her hands, came out of the house. She put the tray down on the table by the swing seat, left.

'Pour,' Ada commanded.

He went over to the table, lifted the bottle of Veuve Clicquot out of the cooler, eased out the cork, filled the flute and passed this to her. As he dropped three cubes of ice into the glass and poured over them a generous amount of Carlos I, he thought how much more acceptable were the crumbs from a rich man's table than the slices of bread from a poor man's. He returned to his seat.

'So now you can tell me what you want to ask Rino,' she said.

'I think it would be best if . . .'

'In my house, it's what I think is best that's best.'

'I'm afraid that cannot always be true.'

'You've a hell of a gall for a little country detective.'

'It's all I have, so I guard it carefully.'

'Do you now! Arrive uninvited, hang out your tongue, and then try to tell me you can do as you like in my house!'

There had been no anger in her voice, only amusement. He congratulated himself on correctly judging her character.

She picked up the bottle of champagne and refilled her

glass. 'Are you still daft enough to think he knows something about Sabrina Ogden's disappearance?'

'It seems possible.'

'It's impossible.'

'How can you be so certain?'

'He's here because he amuses me and I give him a life of luxury. But I've known what it is to be hard up and looked down on by almost everyone, so I always want a quid's worth for every quid I spend. Are you with me?'

'I think I understand.'

'I'm telling you he knows that if he started to mess around with another woman, I'd kick him out.'

'Can you be sure he understands that? In my job, I meet people who could know the truth, but don't because they don't wish to. Even if he should be certain how you would react to his engaging in such a friendship, he might be able to hide that certainty from himself.'

'His mind doesn't have that sort of a kink.' She drained her glass, refilled it. 'People laugh at me. But even the worst of the local snobs can't call me a fool. Someone like him can have the women swarming, so I've always kept both eyes wide open. I'm telling you, that whenever the two meet, he doesn't respond.'

'You are suggesting that Señora Ogden finds him attractive?'

'Married to Bevis, any red-blooded man would seem attractive.'

'He's never responded? Many men would, since she is beautiful.'

'If their women are stupid enough to trust 'em out of sight.'

'Do you know of any man who has been paying her unusual attention?'

'What a refined way of asking if some randy bastard has been after her goodies!' she sneered.

'I have heard that Señor Keane was friendly with her.'

'It's possible, seeing the mouse of a wife he's got. But I don't know and I don't care. What other people get up to is their shout and good luck to 'em if they get away with it.'

'Señorita, I need to ask you where Señor Ruffolo was on

Sunday afternoon, the sixth – which is when the señora disappeared – and all the following Monday?'

'Where d'you think he was? Here, with me.'

'You did not enjoy a siesta on either day?'

'No.'

'Was that not unusual?'

'Why d'you keep on asking bloody stupid questions? Is it your weaselly way of saying what you think of me having a boyfriend young enough to be my son?'

'The relationship is no concern of mine. But were I to consider it, I would say that since it obviously gives you pleasure, you are to be envied, not criticized.'

'I'll tell you one thing, that's a different way of looking at things! The local expats look down their noses at anyone who so much as drops an aitch, so they reckon I'm dirt. Of course, that doesn't stop 'em coming here and eating my grub and drinking my booze because it's better than anything they can afford at home. There's no bigger freeloader than the upmarket Brit.'

'I am a peasant; peasants accept the world as it is.'

She refilled her glass yet again, looked across. 'Why aren't you drinking? The brandy's not good enough for a peasant?'

He drained his glass, picked up the bottle of Carlos I.

Despite an urbanizacíon of small, boxy houses along one side of the easterly inlet in the bay, which suggested architects and planners were blind as well as artistically insensitive, Cala Roig remained attractive thanks to sandy beaches, clear water, and a backdrop of stark mountains which plunged down into the sea.

Alvarez parked in front of the Hotel Azul and climbed the stairs to the main entrance, to be met by Maitland in the foyer. They walked through to the terrace, built sufficiently high that the road below was not readily visible and the view was of sky, sea, and mountains.

Once seated, Maitland gestured with his hand. 'Can you find anywhere more beautiful than this?'

'Before . . .' Alvarez stopped.

'You were going to say?'

'It was even more beautiful when there were no hotels or houses for tourists, and only fishermen walked the sand. But perhaps to speak like that is to speak stupidly. In the past, those who lived here worked the fishing boats and so knew too much hardship to lift their eyes to the beauty and so it could be true to say there was none.'

'It has to be appreciated to exist? . . . Was life that hard?'

'For most. So maybe it is the ugly hotels and the even uglier houses which have banished poverty which are truly beautiful.'

Maitland smiled. 'That's a novel way of looking at things!'

A waiter came to their table and took their order.

Maitland said: 'Have you heard from Son Jordi?'

'From where?'

'Isn't that where Belinda Ogden supposedly died?'

'I'm sorry, my mind was still in the past . . . No, there's been no word yet.' There was hardly likely to be. It was only the previous day that Salas would have asked for inquiries to be made; with the weekend approaching, no one was going to rush to carry out a request from another province . . .

'I guess it's bound to take time to identify the people concerned.'

'There can always be problems.'

The waiter brought them their drinks, spiked the bill, left.

Maitland raised his glass. 'Health, wealth and happiness.' He drank. 'Would you agree that as far as the problem of the missing Sabrina is concerned, for the moment we're at a standstill?'

'I think that has to be accepted.'

'Ogden will continue to deny anything and everything; without the physical presence of Sabrina, we cannot prove she is also Belinda; until the death certificate has been confirmed as false, officially we have to accept it as true . . . It all adds up to the unwelcome fact that I can't justify staying on here and must make for home. There, I'll do what further checking I can, but Ogden will have covered every contingency he could think of.' Maitland paused, then spoke more cheerfully. 'Still, even if it can never be legally proved that Belinda's death was a sham, at least we'll have spiked Ogden's guns – now, he'll never dare try to claim under Sabrina's life policy.'

CHAPTER 14

The second day of the Llueso festival was proceeding as planned. The Moors had suffered their heaviest defeat for many years and three were in hospital while only one Christian had suffered a wound needing medical attention. That evening there would be a display of Mallorquin dancing and, for those of strong disposition, a competition for Mallorquin bagpipes. Finally, there would be dancing in the square to the music of a pop group which would ensure that only those inhabitants who lived on the outskirts of the village could hope to enjoy any sleep.

Traffic had been barred from the old square and there was no parking in the roads leading up to it. After driving around for ten minutes, Alvarez finally accepted that he was going to have to park well away from the post. Swearing, he left his car and made his way through the narrow, twisting streets, keeping to the shade wherever possible.

Once in his office, he slumped down in the chair, stared at the closed shutters, and wondered why life was pain. Then, gradually, as he regained his breath, ceased to sweat, and the relative coolness and peace worked their charms, he relaxed and accepted that life did still have pleasures to offer. Because it was a Saturday, work finished at lunchtime; because it was the fiesta, Dolores would be cooking something special and lunch might well be one of those meals which warmed a man's memory for years after the event . . .

The phone rang and it was in a carefree spirit that he reached for the receiver. Which went to prove that a man was most likely to fall into a hole when he was looking up at the stars.

'You'd better come quick.'

'What's the trouble?'

'The bloody dog went off and wouldn't come back.'

If the speaker thought he was in the business of finding lost dogs . . . 'What's your name?'

'Marcos.'

'Your surname?'

'Coll.'

'Do you know the penalty for wantonly wasting the time of a member of the Cuerpo General de Policia?'

'No, and I bloody well don't care. And if you're not interested in the body, who is?'

'What body?'

'Haven't I been trying to tell you and all you can do is go on about wasting time? The dog went off and I could hear it barking, but it wouldn't come back when I shouted. So I had to climb up through the woods to find out what was going on and there it was, barking at the body in the bushes.'

Sweating profusely, seriously short of breath and hoping that if a heart attack were imminent it would carry him off before he was aware of the fact, convinced that Coll, the older by many years, was deliberately setting a ridiculously fast pace as a derisive, two-finger gesture, Alvarez stumbled his way up through the pine trees.

The naked body was not visible until he was within a couple of metres of it because of the undergrowth. She lay, half curled up, one arm outstretched. Sabrina Ogden? It was impossible to be certain from looking at her, she had been so savaged by time, but if it was she then obviously the BMW at the airport, with the crumpled-up receipt in the well, had been a plant to make it seem she had left the island alive . . .

'Been there quite some time,' said Coll, interested but not shocked. He had lived in times when there were so many tragedies that only those which directly affected one were of any consequence.

Death, Alvarez thought sadly, became twice as obscene when it occurred in the midst of great natural beauty. Because they were at a height of roughly four hundred metres, they could look out and see almost the whole of the Llueso plain, the bay, the sea . . . 'She's likely to have been here close on a month.'

'You know her, then?'

'Probably a missing Englishwoman. Have you searched the area?'

'What would I do that for?'

'So when you were looking for your dog, you just walked up the way we did now?'

''Course I did. Ain't stupid enough to go in circles.'

'Do you often come up here?'

'Ain't no cause to.'

'Would anyone else have reason?'

'There ain't no one else works on the estate but the wife, and she don't.'

'You'd better give me a hand making a quick search before I call the doctor.'

'He'll be a funny sort of doctor if he can do her any good.'

'He'll be acting as a pathologist.'

They found nothing of any significance in the open area, or on the pine-covered slopes which surrounded this. Alvarez unwillingly climbed up until he was above the sheer face of rock and then, showing a courage that only he or someone else suffering from altophobia could begin to appreciate, approached the edge to search the area from which it was reasonable to assume she had fallen. The rock could not record impressions, what earth there was was too hard to do so; only some dried, dead grass, torn from its roots and blown up against brambles, suggested where she might have stood and then, as she began to fall, scrabbled desperately with her feet to try to regain her balance.

He carefully made his way down to where Coll waited, his dog, a poor example of an Ibicenco hound, now at his side. 'Is there a phone in the house?'

'No. But the señor made me have a mobile. Bloody thing! If I had a peseta for every time he's on it to find out what I'm doing and how I'm doing it, I'd be a rich man.'

'Where is it?'

'In my car.'

'Let's get down there.'

Son Brau was a manorial house, a survivor from the past when a few families had possessed considerable wealth and had employed many people to run their estates. Alvarez stared up at the front where recent and extensive repairs could immediately be identified by the different-coloured stone. 'They're working on it, then?'

'The builder says the reformation's cost sixty million so far and there's a long way to go.'

'Is it still the Zafortega family?'

'A cousin to them what did own it.'

'He must be a wealthy man.'

'He's a deeper pocket than you or me, that's for sure.'

'Doesn't live here from what you were saying?'

'He's a huge place in Palma – one of them palaces. Comes out weekends in the summer with the family and gives parties which has the wife working herself into the ground because he won't employ anyone else for the day. They always say that the meanest sod is the richest.'

'Still, he is looking after the place. It's good to know there are people willing to spend to preserve the past.'

Coll shrugged his shoulders. Neither the past nor the future concerned him, only the present.

'Where's your car?'

He led the way round the side of the house to where outbuildings, in a state of disrepair, formed a rough square. He brought out a mobile phone from the Suzuki parked there and handed it across.

After speaking to the local doctor, who was licensed to carry out forensic work, the undertakers, and the photographer, Alvarez phoned Dolores to tell her what had happened and to explain that he would strain every sinew to return in time for lunch, but should he be unavoidably detained, would she make certain a meal was set aside for him.

The doctor walked back to where Alvarez stood. He hesitated, then said: 'Wouldn't have a cigarette, would you? I'm supposed to have given 'em up, but after a job like that . . .'

Alvarez brought a pack out of his pocket, lit a match for

both of them. 'Have you learned anything?' he asked, as he dropped the spent match on to the ground and then stamped on it to make certain there could be no chance of setting fire to the tinder-dry undergrowth.

'Only the obvious – that she fell on to her head.' He smoked, drawing on the cigarette with nervous frequency.

'Can you judge how long she's been dead?'

'In this heat, it's impossible to say any more than probably between three and six weeks.'

'There's been only one report of a missing woman in that time . . . Señora Ogden.'

'There's no wedding or engagement ring, but her left arm was under her and the skin has survived sufficiently well to show she normally wore rings on her third finger.'

'They would have been taken off for the same reason she was stripped of her clothes – the murderer hoped that this was such an isolated spot that either she would never be found, or not until her body was in such a state that there would be no identification unless there was probable certainty as to who she might be . . . Until now, there's been every reason for accepting that Señora Ogden left the island at the beginning of July.'

They heard the sounds of approaching people; led by Coll, five men appeared. Alvarez spoke to the photographer, who owned a shop in Llueso and was under contract to work for the police, and explained what shots he wanted. When these had been taken, the dead woman was put in the body bag which was placed on a stretcher and carried away.

After the doctor left, Alvarez went over to the crushed bushes, dead weeds, and grass which marked where the body had lain. He pulled on a pair of stout rubber gloves and began to search, inch by inch, for anything which might be of some significance.

Coll's dog appeared and started growling; Coll stepped into sight. 'It won't hurt you.'

'Have you told it that?' Alvarez said, as he straightened up.

Coll sniggered, but finally shouted at the dog, who slunk away, its tail down. 'What are you doing?'

'Searching.'

'What for?'

'I don't know.'

'Then how will you tell when you've found it?'

Alvarez resumed his search.

CHAPTER 15

Ogden stared at Alvarez. 'No,' he shouted. 'It can't be. I won't believe it.' He ran out of the sitting-room.

Alvarez sat in one of the armchairs and stared through the window at the tree-covered hills. The hardest task for a policeman was to have to carry grief to someone. Ogden's reactions suggested he had been overwhelmed by grief. Or was he a good actor? Time would probably tell which was the truth.

Eventually, Ogden returned, red-eyed, slightly unsteady on his feet. He slumped down on a chair. 'You're wrong.'

'I sincerely hope so. But you've not heard from her since the Sunday, have you?'

'No.'

'Then since I have to do what I can to identify the dead woman, and very sadly it seems possible . . .'

'Sabrina's car was at the airport. The last time you were here, you went on and on that she'd flown from the island.'

'Yes, I know, but . . .'

'You and Maitland were accusing me of being a crook, trying to say my beloved Belinda hadn't really died, even though I had the death certificate . . .' He seemed to lose the thread of what he was saying and for a moment he stared vaguely at Alvarez. Then he cried wildly: 'It can't be her.'

'As I have said, señor, I hope it is not, and the quickest way of making certain is to find her fingerprints somewhere in this house and compare them with those of the dead woman.'

Ogden mumbled: 'I need a drink,' and began to stand, caught his right foot on something and tumbled back on to the chair.

'It will help us both if you do not have another drink for a while.'

'If I want one, I'll have one.' Despite his belligerent words, he remained seated.

'I need something which the señora will have handled, but will probably not have been cleaned since she disappeared. Does she have a toilet-set – a brush, a hand mirror?'

'Yes.'

'Would Concha clean them regularly?'

Ogden did not answer, and Alvarez repeated the question.

'My wife keeps them in a drawer of her dressing-table because they're silver backed.' There was a pause. 'Can't be too careful with servants around.'

Alvarez knew brief, contemptuous anger. Concha might be a fool of a woman when it came to men, but one could leave her alone in a roomful of ten-thousand-peseta notes and not one would ever be taken. 'Will you show me, please?'

'What d'you mean?'

'I wish to find if they might have the señora's prints on them.'

'Why?'

Alvarez explained in simple terms, much as he would have done if speaking to a child, and eventually Ogden took him through to a large bedroom that was furnished in very feminine style. The kidney-shaped dressing-table had three drawers and Ogden pulled open the centre one and was about to reach inside when Alvarez stopped him. 'Please leave it to me, señor.'

'I thought you wanted to see the mirror?'

'If you'll move . . .' Holding the hand mirror by the edges, Alvarez lifted it out; luckily, from his point of view, it was of modern style and had a plain silver handle and back. In the small case he'd brought with him were a bottle of dusting powder, a brush, a roll of low-adhesive tape, several squares of clean white card, and a newspaper. He opened out the newspaper on the top of the dressing-table, placed the mirror on its front in the centre of this. He repeatedly dipped the brush into the powder and drew it across the back of the mirror, and a jumble of prints became visible. He laid a strip of tape across one section of the back, then placed the tape, adhesive side down, on a white card; he repeated this until he'd covered the whole area. That done, he carried out the exercise on the handle.

Ogden, who'd been silent, suddenly said violently: 'You'll find it's not her.'

'I hope so,' Alvarez replied yet again. He carefully packed everything in the case. 'What jewellery was your wife wearing on the Sunday she disappeared?'

'God Almighty! You think I can remember that?'

'Then you can't be certain whether or not she was wearing engagement and wedding rings?'

'She never took them off.'

'Can you describe them?'

'What d'you mean?'

'Was the wedding ring gold or platinum, did it bear any kind of dedication, was the engagement ring a diamond one?'

'What's all that matter?'

'Since the dead woman had no rings on her fingers, though her skin showed she usually wore them, it seems every means was taken to make her identification impossible and so should . . .' He stopped as Ogden ran out of the bedroom.

As he patiently waited, he heard the faint clink of glass against glass and wondered if Ogden were drinking from anguish or fear?

It was several minutes before Ogden returned, and as he entered the bedroom he suffered a moment of unsteadiness and had to grip the opened door to maintain his balance. 'What d'you want now?' he asked shrilly.

'I am waiting for you to describe your wife's rings.'

Ogden went over to the bed and sat heavily, stared at the floor, his mouth slightly open so that a dribble of spittle began to slip down his chin.

'Is the señora's jewellery insured?' Alvarez asked.

'Yes.'

'Do you have the insurance papers?'

'Yes.'

'Perhaps you will get them for me?'

'Why?'

'They will describe the rings.'

Ogden seemed bewildered, but after a while he staggered to his feet and left the bedroom. Again there was the clink of glass before he returned. He lurched forward as he held out a folder, then collapsed on to the bed.

Alvarez checked through the papers in the folder, found the policy issued by a British company which covered jewellery. Listed amongst the pieces were a platinum wedding ring, a Victorian square emerald-and-diamond ring, and an Art-Deco sapphire-and-diamond ring, the last two both with an insured value of twelve thousand pounds. 'Is the señora's engagement ring the emerald or the sapphire one?'

It was a full minute before Ogden mumbled: 'She wanted a sapphire because her mother had one for her wedding . . .' He became silent.

Alvarez replaced the policy in the folder and held that out, but Ogden made no move to take it so he put it down on the bed. 'Thank you for your help.'

There was no response.

Alvarez left. He climbed into the car, wondering how there could be those so blind to true value as to spend millions of pesetas on jewellery rather than on hectares of rich soil.

It was only when Alvarez checked in the telephone directory that he realized he had forgotten to ask Coll for Zafortega's address in Palma, which meant that since there was no land phone to Son Brau, he could not readily identify which of the Zafortegas listed was the owner of the property. Acting on the principle that he'd live in one of the best areas, he dialled a likely number, only to be curtly informed that the speaker was not the owner. It was, he thought, odd how the wealthy so often distanced themselves with rudeness; perhaps they were scared that politeness would be mistaken for the suggestion of equality. His second call was luckier.

'Yes?' said a man. 'What is it?'

He pictured the other as balding, pot-bellied, and scented with cigar smoke. 'My name is Inspector Alvarez of the Cuerpo General de Policia. Are you the owner of Son Brau?'

'And if I am?'

'Then I regret to have to inform you that the body of a woman has been discovered on your estate.'

'Indeed.'

He had sounded rather as if he had been informed that the pine trees were in flower in the autumn instead of the spring; odd, but not his concern. 'It was roughly a kilometre from the house . . .'

'Who is she?'

'Her identity has not yet been established. Her body was lying at the foot of a natural wall of rock, roughly eight metres high, which backs a relatively flat area – perhaps you know where I'm talking about?'

'I am not in the habit of tramping through the woods.'

Only a man blind and deaf to the true values of life could own such land and not walk every centimetre of it. Yet that morning he'd been praising Zafortega for reforming the house and so keeping the past alive. An example of the contradictions in every human mind, or proof that the true motivation for the reformation was the urge to display wealth?

'What was she doing on my property?'

'I don't yet know. But it may help me to find out if you will tell me something. Do you know Señor and Señora Ogden?'

'Why do you ask?'

'It is possible that Señora Ogden is the dead woman.'

'A moment ago, you informed me that you did not know who she was.'

'I think I said that her identity had not been established. Señora Ogden disappeared a month ago and although the evidence suggested she had left the island, lacking definite proof of that fact, one has to accept the possibility that she did not. No other woman has recently been reported missing, and although it is impossible to judge with any great accuracy how long the woman has been dead . . .'

'I am far too busy to have the time to listen to irrelevances.'

'I'm sorry, señor, but I was trying to explain why I asked if you knew the Ogdens.'

'I have met them. My wife is very broad minded and receives the British.'

'Would they have visited you at Son Brau?'

'Yes.'

'Then Señor Ogden may well have walked around the estate?'

'When the English are not drinking, they often exercise. Is that all?'

'I think so. May I thank you, señor . . .' He stopped when the connection was cut.

He phoned Salas's office and spoke to an assistant who told him that neither the superior chief nor his personal secretary was present; however, there was a number through which Salas could be contacted in an emergency. Since this started with 908, signifying it was a mobile, he wondered as he dialled if Salas was at the nineteenth hole . . .

'Alfredo Salas speaking.'

'It's Inspector Alvarez . . .'

There was an immediate change of tone. 'Who gave you this number?'

'Your office, señor, when I explained that I needed to contact you because the body of a woman has been found and you had to be informed immediately . . .'

'Found where?'

'On an estate called Son Brau which belongs to Señor Zafortega . . .'

'Claudio Zafortega?'

'I'm afraid I don't know his Christian name.'

'Naturally, since that is important! If the person in question *is* Señor Claudio Zafortega he is a man of very great importance and I should have been informed the moment the whereabouts of the body was reported so that I could take charge of the investigation, thereby avoiding the confusion that inevitably follows any that you conduct.'

On Monday morning, an assistant at the Laboratory of Forensic Sciences made an initial report over the telephone. 'We were able to raise prints, with the help of someone from Forensic Anatomy, and these show a sufficient number of matching characteristics with the comparison prints you provided to make identification certain; the dead woman is Sabrina Ogden.'

After ringing off, Alvarez considered the significance of what he had just learned. Sabrina had not flown from the island, although considerable ingenuity had been used to make it seem that she had. Had she been murdered? In view of the missing clothes and rings, that might seem a ridiculous question. But, remembering all the circumstances, it was within the realms of possibility that she had had an assignation – with a lover, with an accomplice – and had suffered an accident; that then she had been stripped and her rings had been removed in an effort to ensure that if her body were found, she would not be identified so it would continue to be assumed that she had left the island.

Motive was a keystone to a planned murder, its presence as significant as its apparent absence. Half a million pounds provided a strong motive, jealousy, likewise. Put the two together . . .

Had Ogden good reason to be jealous?

CHAPTER 16

Alvarez drove to Ca'n Nou, and, as he stepped out of his car, Ogden hurried out of the house. 'Have you found out?' he shouted. 'It's not her, is it?'

'I have just heard from Palma, señor. Very sadly, the finger-prints I recovered here the other day confirm that the dead woman is your wife.'

Ogden stared at him for several seconds, then began to shout incoherently; he turned and ran into the house. Concha appeared in the front doorway. 'What is it now?' she demanded angrily. 'What have you been saying to him?'

'That it is certain the dead woman up in the mountains was his wife.'

She crossed herself. 'No wonder he is crazed.'

He turned and walked to his car. Throughout the drive to Parelona he tried, and failed, to decide whether Ogden had been overwhelmed by grief or fear.

The front door of Ca Na Ada was opened by a young woman, in maid's uniform, whom he had not met before. Ripely attractive, she had not yet begun to gain weight, the fate so many Mallorquin women suffered in the middle or late twenties. 'Is Señor Ruffolo at home?' he asked.

'No.'

'Is Señorita Heron?'

'They're both away. Spending the night in France because of some exhibition or other and won't be back until tomorrow, midday.'

'I'm Inspector Alvarez. And you are?'

'Inés. You've been here before, haven't you?'

'That's right.'

'Marta said something was up.'

He did not answer the unasked question. 'Would you have

time for a chat?'

'I've finished all the cleaning, so there's nothing much else to do. You'd best come in.'

He stepped into the hall.

'Would you like a coffee?'

'I would.'

'Then come on through to the kitchen.'

Nothing could more starkly epitomize the difference between the past and the present than a comparison between the kitchen in which his mother had cooked and this one. She had had an open fire, a charcoal cooker, and a sink which lacked running water; here, there was a double electric oven, a ceramic hob, a double sink with hot and cold running water, a refrigerator large enough to serve several families, a deep freeze, and an array of electrical equipment that would not have disgraced a show window.

'How about a coñac?'

'An excellent idea!'

She smiled, prepared a coffee machine.

'This is the life when you've won El Gordo!'

'It's all right, I suppose.'

'But not what you'd choose?'

'I'd go somewhere where there's some life; there's none out here.'

'Don't they still have dances at the hotel?'

'Not for the likes of me.'

'If you had the money, they'd be for the likes of you. There's not much that money can't do for one. I guess Ruffolo knows all about that?'

'Him!' She switched on the coffee maker, crossed to a cupboard and brought out a bottle of Soberano and a glass, put both on the table. 'Help yourself.'

He poured himself a drink. 'Is there any ice?'

'More than you'll want.' She opened the left-hand door of the refrigerator and brought out a container of ice cubes which she put down on the table.

He dropped three cubes into the brandy. 'Ruffolo's a lucky man.'

She made no comment.

'Do I get the impression you don't like him?'

'Doesn't matter whether I do or don't, does it?'

'Just interested. I reckon to be able to judge a person fairly accurately and I'd say he can be a bit of a bastard.'

She was obviously surprised by that comment. 'He likes himself, that's for sure.'

'And he likes the ladies?'

'Maybe he does, but when the señorita's around, he keeps those kind of likes to himself.'

'She watches him closely?'

'If he so much as looks twice at another woman at a party here, she's telling him to look elsewhere. Which is really funny, considering –' She stopped abruptly.

'Yes?'

'Nothing.' She crossed to the refrigerator. 'D'you want milk or cream?'

'Milk, thanks. What's he like with you three?'

She didn't answer as she put a small jug of milk in front of him.

'Good at giving orders, I'd think?'

She spoke with sudden venom. 'He lives off her, yet with us he acts like a great hidalgo.'

'I'm not surprised. Still, I'm sure you don't take much notice of him?'

'That depends if she's around.'

'He complains about you to her?'

'The other day, the señorita said the windows in the sitting-room needed cleaning and I was to do 'em right away. Then he turns up and can't find a book, says one of us must have moved it and I'm to find it. I said, couldn't *he* look as I was so busy? I mean, it wasn't asking much. He told the señorita I was rude to him. She went for me all ends up. I couldn't understand much of what she was saying, but it must have been nasty or he wouldn't have been smirking so hard. I can tell you, if she wasn't all right to work for and didn't pay better than most, and if I wasn't saving so me and my novio can get married, I wouldn't put up with working in the same place as him.'

The coffee machine hissed and she switched it off. She filled two mugs, pulled up another chair and sat.

'Aren't you going to have a drink?' he asked.

She shook her head. 'Don't really like it. But you have some more if you want. The señorita lets us have what drink we want, though not the same quality as hers, of course.'

'She seems a more pleasant character than he is.'

'Maybe she's a stupid old woman to pander to him like she does, but if he's not involved, she never treats us as if we were dirt. Maybe it's silly, but I sometimes wonder if she's sympathetic because she knows what life's like working for someone who's rich when you have to watch every peseta.'

'That's certainly possible.'

'Kind of makes me feel sorry for her.'

'Because of the way he repays her?'

She sipped the coffee, then added more sugar.

'I suppose that when she's not watching him closely enough, he's ploughing other fields?'

She looked uneasily at him, surprised he had understood what she hadn't said.

'Have you actually seen him with other women?'

'It doesn't seem right to talk like this when I take her money.'

He silently applauded her sense of loyalty, while working out how to circumvent it. He spoke obliquely about how justice sometimes called on a person to reveal what normally it would be morally right for her to conceal . . .

Initially, she spoke with great reluctance, but then, having taken the first few steps, she gained confidence and even enjoyed the chance to gossip. It had been Carlos who had reckoned that the pimp – as they'd nicknamed Ruffolo – was doing his duty at Ca Na Ada, but finding his pleasures elsewhere. Look how he often pressed the señorita to drink even more heavily than normal at lunchtime with the inevitable result that her siesta became very prolonged; how, when this happened, he drove away from the house as soon as it was obvious that she was well and truly asleep; how, on his return, he would be unusually pleasant to the staff. She and Marta had jeered at Carlos and said he was imagining things because he'd only room in his head for one subject, but once it had been suggested, they'd started to watch and judge. It was true. The pimp did encourage the señorita to drink so much she did not leave her bed until the evening, he did drive off as soon as he could be certain she was fast asleep, he was almost pleasant on his return. So what explanation could there be other than that he was seeing another woman? . . .

'Have any of you seen him with someone?'

She shook her head.

'Or learned anything to prove your suspicions true?'

'No.'

'No phone calls for him from women you can't identify?'

'Not on the house phone. But he's got a mobile and he'd use that, wouldn't he, so that none of us would know who was calling him . . . Here, you won't let on what I've been saying, will you?'

'Not a word,' he promised.

Back in his office, he spoke over the telephone to a member of Telefonica's mobile service and asked for a list of all calls made by Rino Ruffolo in the past three months to be faxed to him as soon as it could be drawn up.

He had passed his plate to Dolores for a second helping of calderet extremadura de cabrita when the telephone rang. She looked at him and then at Jaime. 'Is everyone deaf?'

'It can't be for me,' Jaime said.

'No one's going to ring me in the middle of lunch,' Alvarez said.

She spoke to Juan. 'Go and find out who it is.'

'Why can't one of them?' Juan asked resentfully.

'Because men are incapable of doing anything other than eating and drinking.' As Juan left, she heaped two large spoonfuls of the kid stew on to the plate, passed this to Alvarez, sat.

Juan returned. 'It's for you, Uncle, even if you said it couldn't be.'

Alvarez spoke through a mouthful. 'So what stupid bastard's ringing at this time?'

110

'The superior chief.' Juan sat. 'Are you going to tell him he's a stupid bastard?'

'How dare you speak such rudeness,' Dolores snapped.

'But that's what Uncle's just said.'

'Which is poor enough reason for repeating it.'

Alvarez went through to the front room, picked up the receiver. 'Señor?'

'Why are you not at work, but at home?'

'It's lunchtime . . .'

'The efficient officer contents himself with a sandwich at his desk.'

Which probably explained why efficient officers were such humourless men.

'I am ringing to inform you that the owner of Son Brau *is* Señor Claudio Zafortega, one of the most important men on the island. He informed me that he had considerable difficulty in understanding what you were trying to say to him. I apologized for your inadequacies and explained that regretfully there still remained in the Cuerpo a few officers who had been appointed in times when the standards of intelligence and education had not been high. In order to make certain he suffers no further embarrassment, should there be need to contact him, you will inform me and I will speak with him. Is that clear?'

'Yes, señor.'

'What progress have you made in the investigation?'

'Right now, I'm not certain.'

'It has never occurred to you that you are required to be certain?'

'What I'm trying to say, señor, is that I may have a fresh lead, but I have not yet been able to follow it up.'

'Spend less time at home eating and you might be more capable of doing your job.' He cut the connection.

Alvarez replaced the receiver. A sandwich for lunch?

When he entered the post, the duty cabo called out: 'There's a fax for you. Came through an hour ago.'

He thanked the other, made his way upstairs and into his room, sat. The fax was a long one and consisted of columns of

111

figures which listed the calls made through Ruffolo's mobile phone. To check through them was a long, boring, tedious task, but at the conclusion he had picked out certain numbers which had been repeated several times. He asked Telefonica to identify the addresses of those numbers.

That evening, as he was about to leave the post, a second fax arrived which listed the addresses. Ca'n Nou was not one of them. So during the past months, Ruffolo had not frequently used his mobile to phone Sabrina when he could be certain that her husband was not at home. He swore. When one had a flash of inspiration, it was only right and proper that it should turn out to have been inspired.

CHAPTER 17

Strangely, it was while he was having his merienda the next morning in the Club Llueso – when his mind should have been resting – that it occurred to him to wonder why Ruffolo should have made so many calls to an estate agent when he was hardly likely to be intending to buy a house.

After a second brandy, to settle his stomach, Alvarez left the club and returned to his car, drove down to the port. The estate agent was one road back from the front and in the two show windows were displayed details of flats, villas, and fincas for sale, every one of which was in English, German, and Spanish, a wonderful bargain. It needed only a very brief study of the prices to confirm that bargains could be expensive. He went in. On the counter were many information sheets and a model of a flat in a block then under construction, sufficiently cleverly presented to make it appear spacious. Behind the counter worked two young women, very different in looks but both smartly dressed and smoothly groomed.

'Can I help you?' asked the blonde in inaccurate and gutturally spoken Spanish.

'Do either of you know Señor Rino Ruffolo?'

The blonde looked at the brunette, the brunette began to fidget with the corner of the keyboard of the PC in front of her.

'Why d'you want to know?' the blonde asked.

'Cuerpo General de Policia.'

'Oh!' She looked away and it became obvious that she was distancing herself as far as possible from whatever was going on.

'I know him,' the brunette finally, and to some extent defiantly, said in slightly better Spanish than her companion.

113

'Your name is?'

'Carol Murdoch.'

'You are English?' he asked in that language.

'Welsh.'

'It will be easier for me if we stick to English!'

She was uncertain whether that was a joke until she saw his smile.

'Has Señor Ruffolo frequently phoned you here in the past weeks?'

'Is there any reason why he shouldn't?'

'None at all. But if he has, I should like to ask you a few questions.'

'What about? Why?'

'Your answers might help me in an investigation I am conducting.'

'Are you saying I've done something wrong?' Worry raised her voice. She kept looking at the blonde for moral support and the latter, uncertain how the situation might develop, carefully refrained from giving it.

'I am here only because you may be able to tell me something I need to know. But since this is not a comfortable place in which to have a friendly conversation, perhaps we could go and find a quiet café where we can talk?'

'I . . . I don't know. I only work mornings and Félix could raise hell if he found I'd gone out.'

'If he is your employer, is he here now?'

She looked at the blonde, who shook her head.

'When we return, I will tell him the circumstances.'

'Then I suppose it'll be all right.' She spoke to the blonde in Spanish. 'If he asks, say what's happened.'

He drove to one of the few cafés in the port which did not cater specifically for the tourist trade and managed to find parking space close by. 'Have you been here before?' he asked, as they stood on the pavement.

She looked at the worn, bleak exterior, shook her head.

He smiled. 'We have a saying, The tastiest lamb may not have the thickest wool. A drink here costs much less than at one of the smart bars on the front.'

The interior was dim, thanks to the very small windows,

dark-coloured and stained wood panelling, and lack of modern lighting; on the walls was hung, in higgledy-piggledy fashion, ancient fishing gear. 'Shall we go over there?' He pointed at a table in the corner.

When she was seated, he said: 'Would you like coffee and something to have with it?'

She asked for a cortado and a dry sherry.

He went over to the bar and ordered a cortado, a coffee with milk, a Tio Pepe, and a Soberano.

'Not seen you around for a while,' said the owner.

'Life's been one long rush.'

'With you sitting on the side watching it go past?'

Alvarez returned to the table and sat. 'Do you smoke?'

'No,' she answered.

'D'you mind if I do?' He lit a cigarette. Because she was, if anything, more nervous than before, he did not immediately question her about Ruffolo, but started a general conversation, asking her how long she'd lived on the island and what had first brought her there. He had the knack, which he now employed to the full, of being able to project a sense of friendliness which almost always provoked a response. By the time the coffee and drinks were brought to the table, she had lost her uneasy reserve and was telling him how she was hoping to buy a small flat if – and it was a big if – she could persuade Félix to forego the usual excessive commission.

He stubbed out the cigarette and judging she was now sufficiently at ease, said: 'Señorita, I must ask you some questions of a personal nature which may disturb you. Please understand that what you tell me will not be repeated to anyone else. Has Señor Ruffolo phoned you on many occasions during the past weeks?'

She nodded as she fiddled with the glass of sherry, now almost empty, twisting it between thumb and forefinger.

'How did you first meet him? How close a friend is he?'

He needed considerable patience to coax her to tell him the facts, yet he judged it was not merely embarrassment that made her reluctant to speak. She had been shopping one afternoon, perhaps three months before, when Ruffolo had started talking to her. Normally, of course, she snubbed any approach from a stranger, but something . . . She tried to explain, then said simply: 'It was electric,' leaving Alvarez to make of that what he could.

They met in the afternoons, whenever he could get away; he'd phone to tell her he was driving over. And she would wait for him . . .

How could she, he wondered, become so deeply enamoured of a man who was interested only in the gratification of his own appetites? Not that she was the only woman to be such a fool. Ada had found him in the streets of Naples and lavished her wealth on him; Sabrina might well have had an affair with him; there would have been others. He possessed the power of a Don Juan, able to seduce in the space of an aria.

He realized his expression had betrayed his thoughts when she said with angry defensiveness: 'The world's not like it used to be. I suppose you think I don't know about the old woman?'

'I have no idea.'

'He told me all about her, soon after we first met. He explained how he'd been living in such terrible poverty that it hurt just to hear about it. When she saved him from that, his gratitude was so terrific, so overwhelming, he determined to do everything he could to repay his debt. That's why he stays with her. It's very noble of him.'

Alvarez could not prevent himself saying: 'You don't think his friendship with you rather contradicts any sense of gratitude towards Señorita Heron?'

'If she doesn't know, how's it harm her? Why are you asking all these nasty questions?'

'Because I am investigating the death of an Englishwoman, Sabrina Ogden.'

She stared at him, her expression shocked. 'God Almighty! You can't think he knows anything about that.'

'It's possible he may be able to assist me.'

'That's absurd!' Then, immediately contradicting this flat denial, she said: 'How could he?'

'Señora Ogden may have told him something that is important, even if he doesn't realize that it is. I have been told that he was very friendly with her.'

116

'That's a lie.'

'How can you be so certain?'

'Because he explained how she just wouldn't leave him alone, but kept on and on . . .'

'Yes, señorita?'

'Can't you guess?'

'I'm afraid not.'

'Trying to seduce him . . . I suppose you think that's funny?'

'Why should I?'

'Because women aren't supposed to behave like that. But she fell for him and that's the way she acted.'

'And he denied her?'

'Sneer away if you want, but the truth is that even though she was attractive, he wouldn't have anything to do with her because she was married.'

Only someone deliberately blind to character, Alvarez thought sadly, could credit Ruffolo with such a sense of honour. 'Why did he tell you about her?'

'Because of the scene.'

'What scene?'

'Does it matter?'

'It might.'

She spoke sullenly. 'I was in the office one morning when he came in . . .'

'When was this?'

'Who cares?'

'It is important.'

'Then I'm damned if I'm going to tell you.'

'Are you afraid that he may know something about Señora Ogden's death?'

'Of course I'm not.'

'Then if it does prove to be important, that can only be to show me how correct you are.'

She finished her sherry.

'Señorita, it will be much easier and more private to tell me here, when only I hear what you say.'

After a moment, she said: 'It was soon after we'd met.'

'What happened when he entered your office?'

117

'He said Ada was at the hairdresser's and would be there for at least an hour and we could go and have a drink. I told him, I couldn't leave the office because of Félix. He started fooling around, trying to make me change my mind. Sabrina saw us and came rushing in. She was like a madwoman. Screamed at him and called me every filthy name she could think of . . . She was so jealous she didn't know what she was doing or saying.'

'How did it end?'

'He managed to calm her down by making her believe that he often joked with me because I was engaged and wouldn't go out and have a drink with him. He left with her. That's all.'

Ruffolo should have remembered that a woman crossed in love was to be feared more than a fighting bull. He stood. 'Let me get you another drink.'

CHAPTER 18

When Carlos opened the front door of Ca Na Ada, Alvarez said: 'Is Señor Ruffolo back from France?'

'He arrived just before lunch.'

'Then I'll have a word with him.' He stepped into the house without waiting to be invited.

Carlos looked annoyed by this breach of decorum, but finally contented himself with muttering: 'He's by the pool.' He left Alvarez to close the door.

Ruffolo, his bronzed body in the briefest of swimming trunks, lay sunbathing on the diving board. Ada, in a costume that highlighted the irregularities of her figure, was on a pool chaise longue in the shade of the complex. As Alvarez approached, she said loudly: 'It must be drinking time.'

He came to a halt. 'On this island, señorita, time is for whatever you wish. I am here to speak to Señor Ruffolo.'

'Why?'

'To see if he can help me in my inquiries into the death of Señora Ogden.'

'Death?'

'The body found in the mountains has been identified as hers.'

She exclaimed with surprise. Then she said with sudden anger: 'Of course he can't bloody well help you.'

'Nevertheless, I have to make certain that he cannot, which is why I must ask him some questions.'

She turned towards Ruffolo and her tone altered. 'Rino, love, he says he must talk to you.'

'Ignore him,' Ruffolo replied with languid contempt. 'Tell him that if he goes on bothering us, we'll complain.'

'Señor, it is your right to complain if you wish,' Alvarez said equably. 'Just as it is my right to ask you questions.

And either I ask them here, or you will return with me to Llueso so that I can ask them at the guardia post.'

There was a brief silence, broken by some good-natured shouting from the beach. Then Ruffolo came to his feet, moving with athletic ease despite the narrowness of the board. He stepped on to the poolside, walked round and past Alvarez, sat on the chair next to the chaise longue. 'Get it over with quickly, then.'

'I would prefer to speak to you on your own.'

'And if I wouldn't?'

'I should begin to think that you are not very intelligent.'

Ada's expression was now so sharp that it held more than a suggestion of viciousness. Ruffolo stood. 'We'll go into the house.'

'But . . .' she began.

'Don't worry, my precious. It's worth the trouble to relieve you of his presence.'

He strode briskly towards the house. Alvarez followed at a more leisurely pace and by the time he stepped into the cool of the sitting-room, Ruffolo was sprawled out on one of the settees. As he shut the outer door, Carlos entered through the inner doorway.

'A gin and tonic and this time make certain there's a slice of lemon in it,' Ruffolo ordered.

Carlos looked at Alvarez.

'He doesn't want anything.'

Carlos left.

Alvarez ignored the arrogant rudeness and spoke pleasantly once he was seated. 'Señor, do you remember my asking you if you were friendly with Señora Ogden?'

'No.'

'Then you will also not remember your answer?'

'That's smart thinking.'

'You said you had only met her casually at parties.'

'So?'

'Would you now like to reconsider your answer?'

'Why should I?'

'You might consider it more advantageous to yourself to be honest.'

120

'I met her, I was polite, and that's the full story. Even if she'd been my type, which she wasn't, I wouldn't have moved.'

'Because of your sense of tremendous gratitude towards the señorita and the desire to express that by denial?'

'Is that supposed to make sense?'

'Surely those are, more or less, your own words?'

Carlos entered and crossed to where Ruffolo sat, put a tall glass down on the occasional table. 'There are two slices of lemon in your drink, señor.'

The words had been spoken deferentially, but Alvarez wondered if Ruffolo possessed even that small degree of self-humility that would have led him to suspect the contempt lurking behind them? He waited until Carlos had left to say: 'Do you remember the circumstances in which you expressed so noble a sentiment?'

'Hardly, since I never spoke such tripe.'

'Then Señorita Carol is a liar?'

Ruffolo could not conceal his sense of shock. 'Who?' he asked weakly.

'Señorita Carol Murdoch.'

'Who's she?'

'She would be very upset to hear you ask such a question. She described the friendship between you and her as very strong.'

Ruffolo drank deeply, looked briefly at Alvarez, stood, walked over to the nearest window and stared out at the pool. 'The fact is . . . I do know Carol.'

'How well?'

He returned to his chair. There was an ingratiating smile on his face. 'You're a man of the world, aren't you?'

'Am I?'

'You can understand that one sometimes needs a little diversion when it can't do any harm.'

'In other words, all the time it remains secret?'

'I knew you'd understand. So there's no need for her to hear about it.' He nodded in the direction of the pool.

'That depends on the truth.'

'I've just noticed you haven't a drink. How typically stupid of Carlos. What would you like?'

121

The blatant opportunism of this sudden hospitality could hardly be missed, but Alvarez had always believed it to be a mistake to hold too firmly to principle. 'A coñac, with just a little ice, please.'

Ruffolo went over to the fireplace and rang the bell, then strolled across to the windows and stared once more in the direction of the pool.

'You have always met the señorita in the afternoons because that is the only time you both are free?'

'I have to be back here when she wakes up. She's terribly possessive.'

'Where do you entertain Señorita Murdoch?'

'That can't matter.'

Carlos entered.

'Why didn't you ask the inspector what he wanted?' Ruffolo asked curtly. 'A large coñac with ice.'

Carlos left.

'The answer does matter, and if you tell me now what it is, perhaps I shall not have to return. Señorita Heron might become even more curious if I did.'

'In . . . in the flat.'

'You have a flat for such occasions?'

'A chap I know rents it and as he's always short of cash . . . He's glad of the extra pesetas.'

'The name of your friend?'

'Hans Wilms.'

'The address of the flat?'

'He won't declare the money so I can't tell you . . .'

'I do not work for the tax people.'

Ruffolo hesitated, then said: 'Fifteen, Carrer Gabriel Font.'

Carlos returned, put a glass down by the side of Alvarez, left.

Alvarez drank, then said: 'Now you have agreed it is more sensible to tell the truth, I will ask you again how well you knew Señora Ogden?'

'You can't think I had anything to do with her death.'

'Until I hear the truth, I have no way of judging.'

'I haven't seen her in weeks and weeks. I swear that's the truth. You've got to believe me.'

122

'Suppose you answer the question I asked?'

'I . . . Well, I did know her quite well.'

'You had an affair with her?'

'It wasn't me who started it. I don't go for married women. But she wouldn't leave me alone.' He saw Alvarez's expression. 'All the women go for me.'

'You must lead a very complicated life. When did the affair start?'

'Maybe a year ago; something like that.'

'And it was still extant when you began an affair with Señorita Murdoch?'

'I didn't say that.'

'Señora Ogden would not have created such a scene in the señorita's office if your relationship with her had come to an end.'

Ruffolo was silent.

'And it continued up to the señora's death?'

'It stopped after the trouble in Carol's place.'

'Are you asking me to believe that Señora Ogden accepted with good grace that she had been supplanted?'

'She was scared at having behaved so stupidly after he . . .'

'Well?'

'Her husband had been asking questions which made her think that perhaps he had heard rumours.'

'Of her affair with you?'

'Yes. So she decided we must bring things to an end.'

'You accepted that?'

'To tell the truth, I had become a little bored. When one has known a woman for a time, there is no mystery left. Don't you agree?'

'Lacking your wide experience, I'd hesitate to do so . . . When was the last time you saw the señora, and this was not at a party?'

'Perhaps a couple of weeks after the scene in the office.' Ruffolo stood and once more looked through the French windows. 'I knew she couldn't stay away for long. There's no need to tell her anything or she'll just become upset. She's such a simple woman.'

Alvarez would have described her as a complicated woman.

Ada entered the sitting-room. 'Gawd, it's a sight cooler in here!' She stared at Alvarez. 'Surprise, surprise, the man's boozing!'

'Señor Ruffolo kindly offered me a drink.'

'And you were too bloody polite to refuse?' She dropped down on to one of the armchairs, her flesh bulging in and around her costume. 'If everyone else is boozing, why aren't I?'

Ruffolo stood. 'I'm sorry, my angel.' He went over to the fireplace and pressed the bell.

'So what have you two men been talking about?'

Ruffolo returned to his chair. 'The inspector has been asking me if I can help in his inquiries into the death of Sabrina.'

'What makes him think you can?'

'As far as I can make out, no particular reason.'

'Then why's he been talking to you and not me?'

'Sweet, how can I possibly answer that? Perhaps he will soon start asking you the same questions he's been asking me.'

'Then in that case, you'd better clear off for a while.'

'I don't understand.'

'He had to talk to you on your own, so he'll need to talk to me on my own. Run along and sunbathe.'

'But . . .'

'Be a good boy.'

Carlos entered the room.

'Champagne for the señora. And another coñac for the inspector. And bring me a gin and tonic out by the pool.' Ruffolo's resentful pique was obvious from his tone.

Ada waited until both Carlos and Ruffolo had left the room, then said: 'All right, let's have it.'

'How do you mean, señorita?' Alvarez asked.

'Don't try and come dumb with me. You may look dozy, but there's a mind behind the face.'

Carlos entered. He put an ice bucket, in which was a bottle of champagne, and a flute on the table at the side of her chair and was about to open the bottle when she stopped him.

'He can do that.' She jerked her head in Alvarez's direction.

Carlos set a full glass down on Alvarez's table, picked up the empty one, left. Alvarez went over to her side and managed to open the bottle of Veuve Clicquot without spilling a drop. He filled the flute, then returned to his seat.

She drank eagerly. 'When I was working and people thought that buying half a pint gave them the right to treat me like a piece of furniture or make suggestions I'd heard a thousand times before, I promised myself that if ever I was rich, I'd drink champagne morning, noon, and night to spit in their eyes. It's not often a dream comes true.'

'Is the reality as satisfying as you'd hoped?'

'That's a bloody funny thing to ask.' She drained her glass, refilled it. 'You're a real cynic, aren't you?'

'I'm old enough to understand life a little.'

'And I'm older than you so I understand more. Which means I know you didn't haul Rino in here just to ask him if he could help you. You reckon he knows something important. What?'

'In any investigation, one hears things that have to be checked out.'

'So what things have you been checking out?'

'Several small matters.'

'Are you going to name them?'

'No.'

'You're a stubborn bastard!'

'We have a saying, When a mule has a Mallorquin owner, it is the mule which swears . . . Perhaps you will confirm that on the Sunday afternoon on which Señora Ogden disappeared, Señor Ruffolo – '

'I told you.'

'You are positive that he was with you then and throughout the Monday?'

'Yes.' She hesitated, then said: 'Is he in trouble?'

'If he has told me the truth, no.'

'He's made me happy.'

'As I have said before, that is all that's important in any relationship.'

'If people have been blacking him, it's only because they're really getting at me.'

'Why should they do that?'

'They're angry that someone like me should be able to lead the life I do. And also because they're scared I can pick out the frauds. Back home, most of 'em were in ordinary jobs, leading ordinary lives, yet out here you'd think they ran the country. So if they get the chance to sneer at me, they give themselves a lift up.'

'If they are so unfriendly, doesn't it make life very unpleasant for you?'

'No.'

'Because you can live in this house which is so much bigger than theirs; you can give parties so much more splendid than they can; they profess to despise you, yet lack the character to refuse to enjoy the kind of hospitality they cannot afford?'

She emptied her glass once more, refilled it. 'You're beginning to scare me. My body is available when that suits me, but I like to keep my mind strictly to myself.'

Keane opened the front door of the bungalow in Ca'n Ximor. He said lightly: 'As predicted, the penny returns.'

Alvarez failed to make any sense of that, but was certain no compliment was intended. He followed the other through to the pool patio where Cora was seated at the table on which were two glasses and a small bowl of stuffed olives. When she saw him, her expression became disturbed.

'An old friend honouring us with a visit,' Keane said.

She mumbled a welcome.

He turned to Alvarez. 'You will undoubtedly join us in a drink?'

He had spoken, Alvarez thought, pleasantly enough, yet it was impossible to escape the impression that behind the words lay sarcasm. 'Thank you; a little coñac with ice would be very pleasant.'

Keane returned into the house. Cora cleared her throat, did this a second time. She tried to smile, but her expression was almost a grimace. 'Have you managed to . . .' She stopped.

'Unfortunately, señora, I have been able to make very little progress in the case. I am hoping your husband will be able to help me.'

'But he can't. You must understand, he can't.'

As she finished speaking, Keane came through the doorway, a glass in his right hand. 'Who can't do what?'

'You can't help the inspector because you don't know anything.'

Keane handed Alvarez the glass. 'I rather thought I'd made that clear at our last meeting.' He sat. 'But perhaps the art of successful detection lies in repeatedly asking the same question until one receives the answer one wants. So what answer would you like from me now?'

'I should prefer to hear the truth.'

'The truth about what?'

'Your relationship with Señora Ogden.'

'He's told you before, there wasn't one,' Cora said, her voice high.

'That's not the answer he seeks,' said Keane. 'So it'll only provoke the same question yet again.'

'I don't understand . . .'

'Because you suffer the grave disadvantage of an innocent mind. The inspector is clearly convinced that I lusted after Sabrina, but she scornfully rejected my advances; that in my jealous, angry resentment, I decided that if I could not enjoy her favours, no one else would get the chance.'

'You're not saying he thinks you . . . Oh, my God! That's impossible.'

'Every detective is trained to believe two impossibilities each day before breakfast.'

She faced Alvarez. 'Can't you understand, my husband didn't even like her?'

'Señora, I have been told differently. You and your husband were friendly with Señora Ogden until he said something to her that caused her immediately to break off the friendship; indeed, she was so upset, she would not repeat even to Señor Ogden what had been said.'

Cora swung round to face Keane. 'Tell him that's just not true.'

Seeking reassurance? Alvarez wondered.

Keane spoke in a typically oblique manner. 'There's no need. Anyone who knew Sabrina could be certain she was incapable of such verbal restraint.'

'The señora,' Alvarez said, 'was silent because she feared that if her husband learned what you had said, he would become so angry there would be serious trouble.'

'Pistols for two, breakfast for one? Not Bevis's scene unless, of course, he could be certain my pistol would misfire.'

'The inference has to be that he would be outraged because you had made an immoral suggestion to his wife.'

'No!' Cora cried. 'Clive couldn't do such a thing.'

'Your support is heart-warming,' Keane said, 'but sadly it's unlikely to carry the weight in the inspector's eyes because a wife's evidence is so often false, intended either to attack or defend her husband.'

Alvarez stolidly persevered with the questioning. 'What did you say to Señora Ogden that so disturbed her?'

'As I've indicated, I've no recollection of any such incident.'

'Even though it caused such offence that it brought an end to the friendship?'

'There was no friendship, merely an acquaintanceship.'

'It's difficult to believe you can't begin to remember what it was you said.'

'Even more difficult to persuade you that the whole incident is almost certainly imaginary.'

Cora said hurriedly: 'You've got to understand, Inspector, that my husband can upset people even though that's the last thing he wants to do. It's just that he's trying . . .' She stopped.

'Yes, señora?'

'To be clever.'

Keane spoke with heavy irony. 'Your character reference has much in common with a gift from the Greeks.'

'But he must understand that if you did say something to upset her, it wasn't . . . You weren't trying to . . . to seduce her.'

'Seduction suggests temptation has to be employed: it's doubtful that, where she was concerned, there was ever any need for this.'

'Why d'you keep talking like that?' she demanded wildly.

'Such unconcern proves my conscience is whiter than the driven snow.'

Alvarez finished his drink. 'Señor, I have just one more

question. Where were you on the afternoon and evening of Sunday, the sixth, and all day Monday?'

Keane shrugged his shoulders. 'I have no idea.'

'It's important to have an answer since Señora Ogden disappeared that Sunday afternoon.'

Cora said wildly: 'Oh, God, you can't really think . . .' She came so clumsily to her feet that her chair fell over. 'I'll find out what we were doing.' She hurried into the house.

Keane leaned over and righted the chair, then said: 'Let me refill your glass.' He stood, picked up Alvarez's glass, went indoors.

Alvarez stared at the distant hills and mountains and watched the shadow of a solitary small puffball of cloud slide along their sides. A couple of dragonflies performed an elaborate dance above the pool. A hummingbird hawk moth, its wings a blur, hovered in front of a lantana bush in flower. A lazy spasm of breeze briefly brought the sounds of the bells of a flock of sheep.

They returned; Cora sat immediately, Keane after he had handed the glass to Alvarez.

Cora said: 'We were in this house the whole weekend.'

'How can you be so certain, señora?'

'It's in my diary.'

'In which,' Keane said, 'the uneventful as well as the eventful is recorded because my wife is a true diarist.'

'May I see that?'

Keane answered. 'As does any lady of an artistic, sensitive nature, my wife records her thoughts and emotions as well as the daily passage of life and therefore all the entries are intensely personal.'

'I only wish to read what is written for those two days.'

'But what thoughts and emotions may my wife have enjoyed or suffered? They are not for sharing with anyone – not even with me.'

'The entries could confirm what your wife has said and then whatever your relationship with Señora Ogden, I would be certain this has no bearing on my investigation.'

'The price of my innocence is the betrayal of her private self? I'm afraid that the cost is too high.'

Alvarez finished his drink, stood and said goodbye. This time, neither of them accompanied him through the house. Was there, in truth, a diary? Did Keane need protection, except from his own tongue? Did his manner indicate merely arrogance, or was it employed as a cloak? Had he pursued Sabrina, only to be scornfully rejected? Did his wife so urgently try to back him up because she wanted to hide from herself the probable truth?

He climbed into the Ibiza and heaved the driving door shut with unnecessary force, his anger sustained by his inability to answer any of those questions either.

CHAPTER 19

Carrer Gabriel Font was in the centre of an area which had been developed over the past few years and thereby done much to destroy the character of the port which had once been its main attraction. Number 15 was a five-storey block of flats, ugly, but not really any uglier than others. The name tag listed Wilms on the third floor. Alvarez pressed the call button of the entryphone. He identified himself and the door lock buzzed.

The lift took him smoothly to the third floor and he stepped out on to a small landing which ran round the central stair shaft and was illuminated by light coming through the cupola above the fifth floor. He crossed to the right-hand door, rang the bell.

Wilms was short, squarely built, and clearly careless of personal cleanliness. 'So what is the problem?' he asked in slow, careful Spanish.

'I'm making inquiries regarding the death of Señora Ogden.'

Wilms finally stepped to one side. The entrance hall was unfurnished except for a large, unframed painting in garish colours whose subject might have been anything or nothing; the sitting-room had paperbacks, magazines, newspapers, and empty cans littered everywhere, while on the table were the remains of at least one meal. Alvarez sat on the chair which looked the least filthy of the three. Wilms lit a cigarette.

'Señor Ruffolo often comes here with a woman, doesn't he?'

'Is that against the law?'

'No. But not declaring the rent that he pays you is,' Alvarez replied, shamelessly forgetting what he'd said to Ruffolo. 'So it'll be in your interests to be helpful.'

Wilms stubbed out the cigarette in an overflowing ashtray, even though it was hardly smoked.

'What do you do when he brings a woman here?'

'Leave. If I'm not here, he lets himself in,' he answered sullenly.

'Have a look at this.' Alvarez passed across the photograph of Sabrina. 'Do you recognize her?'

'Yes.'

'Why?'

'Why d'you think?'

'I'm asking the questions and if they don't get answered, they'll become a whole lot more personal.'

'He used to bring her here.'

'Why d'you say, used to?'

'It's some time since she was around.'

'Have you any idea why?'

'He said they'd decided to call an end to it because the husband was becoming suspicious. With a piece like her, the husband was crazy not to keep his eyes wider open.'

'Perhaps he made the mistake of trusting her. When was the last time you saw her?'

'Quite a few weeks ago; ten, twelve, something like that. Soon after he started bringing the other one along.'

'What was her name?'

'Carol. Much too nice for the likes of him.'

'Has he brought other women here?'

'Yeah.'

'How many?'

'I was only taught to count up to ten. He pulls the birds more easily than I eat breakfasts.'

Alvarez left. As he waited for the lift, he dispiritedly remembered how he had been so certain he had uncovered a second and very valid motive for Sabrina's murder. Under the spur of jealousy, so strong it had deprived her of all common sense, Sabrina had threatened Ruffolo that if he didn't give up Carol, she'd tell Ada about the affair, certain that Ada would respond by throwing him out of her life, not only for his betrayal, but also because he would have made her a laughing stock amongst the expatriate community who must welcome the

132

chance to pour scorn over her. Faced with returning to the poverty of Naples, where his extraordinary attraction for women would almost certainly never regain for him the luxurious life to which he'd become accustomed, he had murdered Sabrina to ensure her silence . . . An ingenious theory which suffered only one drawback, it was based on error. The affair had come to an end when Sabrina had regained a measure of common sense and therefore jealousy would never spur her on to revealing something that would almost certainly destroy her own marriage and way of life.

The lift arrived, the door slid open, and Alvarez stepped inside. As he pressed the ground-floor button, he sadly reflected that there was no bigger fool than the man who prided himself on his own cleverness.

One of Professor Fortunato's assistants phoned him from the Institute of Forensic Anatomy on Wednesday morning.

'We have completed our examination of the body of Señora Ogden. Decomposition was very considerable, as was to be expected, and in consequence our task has been difficult. The cause of death was extensive injuries to the head which resulted in massive brain damage, consistent with a fall from eight metres on to rock. There are no signs of disease, especially any which might upset balance. There are marks on the back in the region of the shoulder blades which could suggest a blow, but these are too indistinct and too corrupted for any definite opinion to be given.

'Sorry to be so negative, but that's the way it is.'

Alvarez replaced the receiver. Experts were meant to resolve questions, but so often they seemed merely to raise further ones. He tapped on the desk with his fingers, thought of many reasons for not ringing Palma, finally accepted that they were all products of his own cowardice. He dialled. The secretary with the plum-filled voice told him to wait.

'What is it?' Salas finally demanded.

'The Institute has just rung me, señor, to say . . .'

'I have already heard from them.'

'This report means we have no confirmation of murder, despite the possible signs of a blow to the back.'

'The fact that she was stripped of her clothes and jewellery means nothing?'

'It is very strong evidence, of course, but it is possible to imagine two alternative explanations.'

'Which are?'

'She met her husband in the woods, knowing the odds were a thousand to one against their being seen there, to discuss how the proposed insurance fraud was progressing. Through carelessness, or ignorance, she fell over the edge. Since the success of the plan depended on her having left the island at the beginning of July, he stripped her body of clothes and jewellery in the hopes that if eventually it were found, it would be in such a state that no great effort would be made to identify it. That, of course, presupposes that if he had heard rumours of her infidelities, he refused to believe them.'

'The second explanation?'

'Perhaps she was naked before she fell and . . .'

'Why should she be?'

'If she had met a man and they were making love . . .'

'Your mind is a sewer.'

'Señor, that is a possibility which fits the known facts.'

'Most regrettably, you seem capable of making even the most innocent of facts fit possibilities that the rest of us are grateful never to envisage.'

There was a short silence, broken by Salas. 'Have you found the time to curb your imagination and pursue more normal investigations?'

'Yes, señor. I have been checking whether there might be an alternative motive to Ogden's for the murder of the señora.'

'Well?'

'I thought I had identified one, but have now discovered this was not so.'

'In other words, a useless exercise.'

'Not really. After all, the absence of something can be as important as its presence.'

'As in the case of intelligence . . . Only Ogden has a motive for the murder of his wife?'

'Yes, señor.'

'Do you intend to arrest him?'

'There is still not the firm evidence that he defrauded the insurance company over Señora Belinda Ogden's death and in my judgement it will be necessary to have that before we arrest him because it will play so vital a part in proving his motive for the death of Señora Sabrina Ogden.'

'Then what are you doing about establishing that proof?'

'Nothing, señor.'

'It does not occur to you that cheerfully making such an admission underlines your inability to do your job?'

'But señor, some time ago you told me not to get in touch with the authorities on the Peninsula, to ask them to investigate the supposed death of Señora Belinda Ogden, you would do that. There's nothing I can do until I hear from them.'

Salas cut the connection.

CHAPTER 20

Alvarez could not have explained why, but the moment he stepped into the house he feared trouble. When he entered the dining-room, his fears were confirmed. Jaime sat at the table, staring disconsolately at an empty bottle of Soberano, Juan was slumped in a chair, Isabel was smirking, and from the kitchen there came the clash of pots and pans.

He sat opposite Jaime, pointed at the bottle, then at the cupboard. Jaime shook his head. 'What's up?' he asked in a low voice.

'Bloody chaos!'

'Why?'

'Ask him.' He indicated Juan.

Alvarez was about to speak to Juan when the bead curtains were imperiously parted and Dolores appeared, head held high, dark-brown eyes glinting, mouth very straight. 'So you're back.'

He uneasily wondered what that remark presaged.

She put her hands on her hips. 'Unlike my husband, do you know why I have a son who is a cheat and a liar?'

'I'm not,' muttered Juan.

'Yes, you are,' jeered Isabel.

'I don't understand what you're getting at.' Alvarez understood one thing. Supper was not going to be a memorable feast.

'So! Because neither his father nor his uncle can look away from a bottle long enough to make certain he learns to behave respectably, he is a cheat and a liar.'

'I'm not,' Juan said, even less forcefully than before.

She faced him. 'Were you not sent back from repaso with a note to your father which I read? Did this not say that it would be impossible for you to reach the necessary standard

136

to go up to the next form in the new term if all you did was fool around and then copy someone else's work? Did it not also say that when you were accused of cheating, you denied this many times, yet the mistakes you made were exactly the same as those made by the girl whose work you were seen to copy? . . . Aiee! What sin have I committed that I have borne a son who will not even finish school, let alone progress to the Institute and university? He will become a beggar. He will end his life in prison, disgracing those who loved him.' She turned on her heels and swept back through the bead curtain.

Jaime looked even gloomier; Isabel's smirk increased; Juan scraped the heels of his shoes across the carpet since he knew this would have annoyed his mother had she been present to observe him.

'What's all this about?' Alvarez asked Juan.

'Nothing.'

'Don't be stupid.'

'He can't help being stupid,' said Isabel gleefully.

'Did you copy from someone else?' Alvarez asked.

Juan shrugged his shoulders. 'Maybe.'

'Why?'

'Because arithmetic bores me.'

'A ridiculous reason. You're doing repaso because if you don't pass the special exams at the end of the holidays, you won't stay with your own age group.'

'I always copy arithmetic from Blanca and she always copies my Spanish grammar. And she's a rotten old cow for telling.'

Alvarez, conscious that Dolores might well be listening to every word, said: 'You must never speak about a lady in such terms.'

'She deliberately made the mistakes so she could laugh at me when I was found out.'

'If you hadn't copied her work, she wouldn't have had that chance.'

'But we agreed to do it like that. Aren't people supposed to do what they promise?'

It was clear to Alvarez that he was not getting the message across and he shifted tack. 'Whatever else happened, you should have told the master the truth.'

'Mother says all men are liars and I'm a man, so why shouldn't I lie?'

Alvarez gave up trying to instil a sense of moral correctness in Juan's mind. He looked at the empty Soberano bottle, thought to hell with it and reached across to open the right-hand door of the sideboard. There was no brandy there. He said in an undertone: 'There's more outside, isn't there?'

'Sure. But are you going to go and fetch it when she's in the mood she is right now?'

Salas's secretary rang at ten-twenty-five on Thursday morning. 'On the orders of the superior chief, you are to proceed to Son Jordi, in the province of Gerona, and there carry out inquiries into the circumstances surrounding the death of Señora Belinda Ogden.'

'I thought –' Alvarez began.

She interrupted him. 'Expenses will be kept to a minimum and every claim must be accompanied by a matching receipt. Is that clear?'

'Not really. I understood from the superior chief that he would be requesting the local Cuerpo to conduct the inquiries. Haven't they done that?'

'Would you be given these instructions if they had?' she said with chilling hauteur before cutting the connection.

The superior chief, Alvarez thought with deep satisfaction, had obviously forgotten at the time to pass on the request; further, the cowardly way in which he had made his secretary give the order now showed that he feared this fact must be obvious.

He took the train from Barcelona to Figueras, there hired a car. He drove along the autoroute towards the border, then turned off and climbed the zigzag road which led, through cork forests, up one of the southerly mountains to Son Jordi, situated on the crown.

It was a village from the past. Obligatory parking was in an open area on the approach. Every house was time-worn and most contained different levels because of the sloping land; the roads were cobbled and so narrow that even mule carts could only traverse them with care; the two shops he passed were the front rooms of houses and sold only the necessaries of life. Then, puffing because walking was hard work, he rounded a corner to come in sight of a group of eight people who could only be tourists because they were dressed with such little regard to decorum. He silently swore. Was not even a hidden corner of Spain to be left unsullied? But as he drew nearer he could hear they were speaking French and his thoughts lightened. With the border so close, it was probable they were in Spain just for the day; they would never have bothered to drive up to a village that boasted no architectural gem or modern tourist attraction unless there was reason; being French, there was a good chance this was a restaurant that offered excellent food.

In fact, there were two restaurants, a couple of hundred metres apart, in the same road. The one which stood higher had a very shabby exterior, the lower one had newly painted shutters and some of the stone work had recently been repaired. He chose the first on the principle that money spent on decoration and repairs did not improve the quality of the food, yet had to be paid for.

Inside was a barn-like area, two floors high, with such small windows that the electric lights had to be switched on despite the fierce sunlight. Tables – many of which were already occupied – were old and wooden, scrubbed so frequently that the wood was whitened; tablecloths were paper serviettes; wine glasses were tumblers; the house wine was served in earthenware jugs. He ordered a brandy and took a long time to choose his meal from a menu offering surprising variety.

The locally caught trout with piquant prawn sauce was memorable in its own right and an apt appetizer for the duck with orange and Cointreau sauce; the chocolate mousse, topped with whipped cream, was so delicious that he ordered a second one to discover if gastronomic miracles were repeatable.

The village, small as it was, had a mayor. Xamena was an old man and dressed, as he had throughout his life, in clothing which would suggest to any official from a town that he was virtually destitute. Slugs always attacked the ripest-looking fruit.

He met Alvarez with such a marked lack of interest that he might not have understood who the Cuerpo were, let alone the possible significance of a visit from one of its members, and it was only with the greatest reluctance that he finally suggested Alvarez enter his house. The front room had – since this was as far as unwanted visitors would progress – been furnished with a couple of uncomfortable chairs, a rush mat that had seen much better days, an ancient cabinet, two yellowing prints, and a miniature Catalan flag.

They sat. Xamena's lower jaw moved as if he were working toothless gums together as he stared vacantly at the rush mat.

'You'll likely have lived here all your life?' Alvarez said.

Xamena was not prepared to make such an admission so early in their conversation.

'Reminds me of the more remote villages our way.'

'Never been to Mallorca.'

'It's a wonderful island . . .'

As Alvarez continued to list the delights of Mallorca, Xamena became uneasy, recognizing his visitor was from the same stock as he and therefore not to be fooled by an appearance of bovine stupidity.

Alvarez switched the discussion – monologue – to agriculture. Was modern apple growing, as practised near the coast, profitable; was the cork industry in decline? Laughingly, he spoke about the farmers who had learned how to work the EU's agricultural policy so firmly to their own advantage that a fallow field became more profitable than one laden with the heaviest crop of corn . . .

Xamena could stand the tension no longer. 'What the hell d'you want?'

Before Alvarez could answer, Xamena's wife appeared through the inner doorway and was about to say something when he roughly ordered her away. For a while, his lower jaw moved more rapidly, then he said hoarsely: 'Is it about the restaurant?'

'You own one?'

He cursed himself for a fool, convinced he was about to learn that income tax was not a myth.

'If it's the top one, I had the best meal there I've had for a long time.'

'There's no profit.'

'The more successful a business, the less profit it makes . . . I've come to ask you something.'

'What?'

'Do you remember an Englishwoman with a man some years back who died in a fall?'

'Are you here because of that?'

Alvarez nodded.

Xamena came to his feet and left the room. When he returned, he carried an unlabelled bottle in one hand and two glasses in the other. 'I've a very small vineyard, very small indeed, and sometimes make a little coñac.'

The brandy, probably made illegally, was rough, but it was the roughness that recalled the past. Alvarez praised it and Xamena refilled his glass.

'As I understand things,' Alvarez said, speaking casually, 'the woman and man went for a walk not really knowing the area?'

'Foreigners would walk over a precipice without seeing it was there.'

'What happened after she'd fallen?'

'He carried her back to the car and drove her down to the doctor at Las Macaulas.'

'Why didn't he bring her here since it would have been so much quicker?'

''Cause there ain't no doctor here and never has been.'

'How d'you think the man knew that?'

Xamena shrugged his shoulders.

'Is the same doctor still practising in Las Macaulas?'

'There's another. And to get him to come up here, you've got to be dying and if you're dead when he arrives, he curses everyone for wasting his time.'

'What happened to the first doctor?'

'Packed in working.'

'He was pretty ancient, then?'

'Him? Wasn't nearing sixty.' Xamena spoke with the scorn of twenty years' seniority.

'Then it was early for him to retire?'

'Always was a lazy sod. So when he come into some money, he said he was fed up with listening to other people's problems.'

'Where did the money come from?'

'How the hell would I know?'

'Does he still live in Las Macaulas?'

'Someone said as him and his family left.'

'Who buried the Englishwoman?'

'Tilo Domingo. He's the only undertaker in Las Macaulas.'

'Has he retired?'

'Hadn't when old Bruno died a few months back. And Catalina, his daughter, said as how the bill was so enormous it was no wonder Domingo had been able to buy himself such a big house.'

The strands were there, Alvarez thought, but would he ever be able to knot them together?

Had he realized how much rough walking was involved, Alvarez would never have arranged for one of the villagers to show him where Belinda Ogden had supposedly fallen. After leaving the car, the five kilometre-trek – his companion swore it was only just over one, but he was trying to make a fool of him – wound up and down precipitous slopes, made dangerous by loose stones and rocks, and he became convinced that he would fall with fatal consequences and have to be driven to Las Macaulas to be buried . . .

The site of Belinda's accident was very similar to that of Sabrina's – a sheer face of rock that backed a relatively level section. The only obvious difference was the lack of any undergrowth. However, there had never been a body to conceal.

CHAPTER 21

Once a small town, Las Macaulas had, thanks to an ever-increasing prosperity, grown into a large town. The centre was a place of haphazardly angled narrow streets and buildings with small windows which gave the impression of an inward-looking population; the new, outer suburbs were laid out geometrically and the houses and bungalows had been built for comfort and many had picture windows so that it seemed that those who lived here looked outwards.

The doctor had lived in an old, slightly crooked house just behind the main street. The new owner had no idea where he'd moved to after retiring, but a nearby chemist thought he'd probably gone to Argentina because he'd often said he wanted to return to where he'd been born only days after his parents had arrived there after fleeing Spain on the success of Franco's army in the Civil War.

Even the most hard-working and dedicated investigator had to accept that he could not work flat out twenty-four hours of the day. And Alvarez had noted a restaurant opposite the market square whose menu had looked very promising . . .

At ten-twenty on Saturday morning, he braked to a halt in front of a large ranch-style bungalow on the northern outskirts of the town. He left the car, crossed the pavement, opened the wrought-iron gate, and walked up a stone path on either side of which was a formally designed garden. The front door was elaborately panelled in very good quality wood. An expensive property.

The door was opened by a woman who was dressed in such style that he became very conscious of the fact he had been wearing the same clothes for a couple of days. He introduced himself. 'I should like a word with your husband, señora.'

'I'm afraid he's at work.'

His brief surprise that a man of substance should work on a Saturday was succeeded by the realization that death did not respect the weekend. He asked for directions to Domingo's office, thanked her, left.

Domingo y Hijos had a single large show window and the display was of a large cut-glass vase filled with flowers, set against a black backcloth; without any obvious indication of the nature of the firm's business, there was no mistaking what that was.

A young woman, well groomed, greeted him in professionally sympathetic tones. She showed him into a room in which the only furniture was six comfortable chairs set in a rough circle, four framed prints, two of religious motifs, two depicting scenes of natural beauty that was touched with sombreness because of dark, heavy clouds, and a deep pile carpet in dark mauve.

Domingo entered. Younger than Alvarez, he was taller, slimmer, and dressed with far greater care. He came forward, hand outstretched. 'My wife phoned to say you would be along. Please sit down.'

Alvarez sat.

'I gather you're from Mallorca. I've visited there twice – a very beautiful island. Of course, there are areas where tourism has unfortunately made itself all too obvious, but if one looks beyond them . . .'

Alvarez listened in silence to the flow of words that was spoken in rich, warm tones.

'That's enough from me. Now, can you say what brings you here?'

'I'm making inquiries concerning the death of Señora Belinda Ogden and it's possible you can help me.'

'That's not a name I recognize. Should I?'

'You were responsible for the funeral arrangements.'

'Indeed. How long ago did she pass on?'

'Roughly three years ago.'

'That's a long time, so it's small wonder I can't recall the sad event. Can you give me any of the details?'

144

'An Englishwoman, in her early twenties, she was walking in the mountains near Son Jordi when she fell and suffered fatal injuries.'

'I vaguely remember such an incident, but no more. No doubt the records will refresh my memory.' Domingo stood. 'Is there a question concerning her death?'

'Yes, there is.'

He waited, but when nothing more was said, left the room. He returned with a file which, once seated, he opened and from which he brought out papers. He skimmed through these, then looked up. 'I remember now. Despite the injuries, a very attractive young woman. Very sad. One always hates to see gilded youth cut down.'

'Are all the records there?'

'Of course. We always keep them longer than the law demands.'

'May I see them?'

Domingo hesitated. 'I don't believe you have explained the reason for your inquiries.'

'I will.'

It was obviously much less of an answer than he'd wanted, nevertheless he handed the file over. Alvarez studied the papers. A printed form filled in with the preliminary details, another which noted that the wishes of the nearest relative concerning the form of interment was still not to hand; a list of expenses which included thirty days of refrigerated storage; a copy of the death certificate; two handwritten letters from Ogden, in one of which he refused to accept any liability for expenses incurred; in the other, he grudgingly agreed to pay them . . . 'I see the husband was reluctant to pay the bill.'

'Was he?'

Alvarez passed the letters across. Domingo read them. 'Of course. It turned out that the man she was with at the time of the accident was a lover and she'd run away from her husband. One could sympathize with the husband's viewpoint, of course, but one does have to observe business terms.'

'What was the name of the man she was with – there doesn't seem to be any mention of it?'

'No? I suppose that when it became clear he was not her

husband and could not meet expenses, there was no cause to note it down. I'm afraid I've no memory of it.'

'The body was collected from the doctor's surgery – how did that happen?'

'As I remember, her companion drove her straight there, hoping something could be done for her. Unfortunately, on arrival she was found to be dead. It naturally became necessary to move the body immediately.'

'Were the police informed of what had happened?'

'I've no idea.'

'They should have been, to check whether it was a genuine accident.'

'I don't think there was the slightest doubt on that score.'

'Who collected the body from the doctor's surgery?'

'We did.'

'Who exactly do you mean by "we"?'

'I have a vague idea that it was one other man and myself.'

'Can you name this other man?'

'No.'

'The circumstances must, to some extent, have been unusual, so probably he will remember the occasion?'

'That could be.'

'Would you speak to all your employees and find out who it was?'

'I'll naturally do what I can, but I have to warn you that he may well have left my employ. People aren't as content to stick to one job as they used to be.'

'Why was the señora cremated?'

'You did not read all of the second letter from the señor? Having reluctantly agreed to meet the costs of his wife's funeral, he said she was to be cremated.'

'Was that unusual?'

'Since the crematorium opened in Barcelona, cremation has become the choice of an increasing number of people, despite the cost of transportation.'

'Chosen especially by someone concerned about the possibility of exhumation?'

'Are you suggesting something?'

'Isn't that obvious?'

'Inspector, you are beginning to talk in riddles.'

'I'll speak more plainly. Whose body was cremated in the name of Belinda Ogden?'

'I don't understand.'

'Who was the dead woman you sent to Barcelona in place of Belinda Ogden's body?'

'Are you suggesting we inadvertently confused bodies? Every body is positively and continuously identified to prevent any such disaster.'

'Nothing was inadvertent.'

'I think you should be more precise in whatever accusation you are trying to make.'

'You were an accomplice in the fraudulent insurance claim following Belinda Ogden's supposed death. Since you could have no control over the cremation – which was essential to avoid exhumation – you did not dare risk delivering to the crematorium a coffin that was filled with something to mimic the necessary bulk and weight because there had to be the thousand to one chance that the deception would come to light. Therefore, you sent the body of another woman, in the name of Señora Ogden, to the crematorium.'

'A suggestion almost as ridiculous as it is insulting.'

'But one which can be tested.'

'Indeed? How?'

'The grave of the woman who should have been buried but was cremated will, on exhumation, prove to be empty.'

'The authorities are naturally always very reluctant to permit a single exhumation on account of the distress caused to the family, yet here you would be asking for not one, but many.'

'Why?'

'Because if I were as clever and crooked as you suggest, when approached to take part in the criminal deception, I would have stipulated that I must arrange the false burial some good while before the cremation so that the identity of the substitute could not later be ascertained by consulting the records of burials immediately before or after the supposed cremation. I can't be certain without checking, but I think you will find that in the month during which the English señora's body was in cold storage, we conducted a considerable number of burials. The authorities will never agree to all of those graves being exhumed.'

Domingo's tone had carried no hint of mockery, yet Alvarez had no doubt that mockery was there. 'How long have you lived in your present house?'

'Not very long.'

'When did you buy it?'

'About three years ago.'

'Quite a coincidence!'

'It is coincidental with what?'

'The supposed death of Señora Ogden.'

'I fail to see any link.'

'Obviously, the money Señor Ogden gave you after the false cremation proved successful enabled you to make the move.'

'You have an ingenious, if somewhat primitive, mind. I wonder how you respond to the fact that I had to take out a mortgage to buy my present home?'

'In one of two ways. It is clearly a very expensive place and the money Señor Ogden gave you was perhaps not sufficient to cover the difference between the cost of it and what you received from the sale of your previous home; that you decided a mortgage would provide good camouflage should anyone wonder at your sudden access to wealth. How much did you get for your previous house, how much did the present one cost, what size is the mortgage?'

'And if I tell you that the answers are solely my business?'

'I inform you that I will arrange for the authority to examine your accounts and bank balances so that from them I can gauge what those answers are.'

'Obviously it will, as so often is the case, be more practical to accede to the wrongful use of authority than to resist it on the grounds of principle . . . There was a convention in England which I went to; whilst there, I bought a lottery ticket. I was returning here before the draw, so I gave the ticket to a charming Englishman I'd met and asked him to check it that Saturday. You can imagine my delight when he rang to say that although I hadn't scooped the top prize, I had won a considerable sum of money. I asked him to send it to me, less five thousand pounds which I hoped he'd accept as a gift – an undeclared token of admiration for his honesty since he could have pocketed everything and I'd never have known. He refused to accept a penny. It's humbling to meet such honesty.'

'I'm sure it surprised you. How did he send you this money?'

'In the literal sense he didn't. He arranged for his bank in the Islas Normandas – I understand that the British are so persecuted by their tax bandits that they find such offshore accounts even more beneficial than we do – to pay it to me when I went there for a short holiday.'

'They gave it to you in what form?'

'A number of high-value travellers' cheques.'

'Where did you cash these?'

'Here and there. I don't really remember.'

'How very convenient!'

'That great philosopher, Javier Solchaga, once said that memory responds to man's subconscious more readily than to his conscious.'

'What is the name of your benefactor?'

'Jeremy Awkright.'

'His address?'

'Very sadly, he passed on soon afterwards. For the truly good, this world is so often a resting place of short duration.'

'Does his widow still live in the same house?'

'I don't remember saying he was married, but, in fact, he was. I had a brief note in reply to my letter of commiseration in which she said she'd found the house too big and full of memories and had sold it and would be moving out within days. She promised to let me know her new address but, sadly, has never done so. I deeply regret that – I should have liked to invite her here for as long as she wished as a small gesture of thanks for her husband's wonderful kindness.'

Domingo had spoken with such warm sincerity that Alvarez found himself almost believing what he had been told.

CHAPTER 22

On Monday morning, Alvarez arrived in his office, sat, and stared at the telephone. He must phone Salas and report on his visit to the Peninsula – an unwelcome task and therefore best carried out as soon as possible. Yet the superior chief might have been delayed by any one of a dozen concerns and not yet at work. So perhaps it was best to wait a while . . .

It was just after ten when he returned from merienda. A task delayed was a task betrayed. He sat, lifted the receiver, dialled.

'Well?' said Salas.

'I have to report, señor, that I questioned the mayor of Son Jordi. I asked him if Señora Belinda Ogden's body had been taken to the village before the undertaker removed it. As expected, it had not been. It seems the señora's companion carried her from the place of the accident to the car and drove her to Las Macaulas.'

'The man's name?'

'I was unable to determine that.' He paused, but surprisingly, Salas made no comment. 'At the doctor's surgery in Las Macaulas, she was pronounced dead. In view of the circumstances, it was necessary to remove her body immediately and the undertaker, Domingo, was called. According to his records, the señora's body was held in storage until Señor Ogden agreed to meet all funeral expenses. He asked for her to be cremated.

'Inquiries in Las Macaulas showed that soon after these incidents, the doctor retired, though not of a retiring age, and left the town with his family. No one knows for certain where he's gone, although there is the suggestion it was Argentina where he was born. I judge it very unlikely that we will be able to trace his present whereabouts.

'I questioned Domingo. I would describe him as smooth as butter, as sharp as a knife, as twisted as a . . .'

'Try not to become absurd.'

'Yes, señor. I asked him to identify the man who, with him, collected the señora's body from the surgery. He claimed this was impossible. He showed me the señora's file which contained two letters from Señor Ogden, the first refusing to pay her funeral expenses, the second agreeing to do so and demanding cremation. There was also the receipt from the Barcelona crematorium. This surely means that when a suitable body became available, a coffin filled with something was buried in the local cemetery, while the body was held back to be sent, when the time was judged right, to the crematorium in the name of Señora Ogden.'

'How much of this does Domingo admit?'

'None of it.'

'An exhumation will prove or disprove the possibility.'

'He pointed out that since it would be impossible for us to pinpoint which of many funerals was faked, many exhumations would have to be undertaken; that the authorities would never agree to this, not least because we can offer only a theory and not proof.'

'If this deception was carried out, Domingo will have demanded and been paid a considerable sum of money. An examination of his lifestyle and accounts will expose this.'

'That's what I reckoned, señor, especially on finding that he'd moved into a new and very expensive house soon after the señora supposedly died. But he claims he won a considerable sum of money on the English lottery and it was that, together with a mortgage, which permitted him to buy the place.'

'Winning money is every criminal's favourite explanation for sudden wealth.'

'He says he bought the ticket in England when attending a conference. Because he would be leaving the country before the draw, he gave the ticket to an English friend he'd met. At a later date the friend phoned him to say he'd won a prize . . .'

'That proves he's lying. The friend would have said nothing so that he could keep the money for himself.'

'But there are people so honest that . . .'

'Spare me such naive stupidity.'

'He claims that the friend transferred the money to a bank in the Islas Normandas and he collected it from there in the form of travellers' cheques. He cannot remember at which bank or banks he cashed these.'

'I've never before heard such a farrago of nonsense.'

'Quite so, señor. But unfortunately, while we can be certain that that is so, it's going to be very difficult to prove this . . .'

'I should have placed the investigation in the hands of the local officers instead of expecting you to handle a matter requiring intelligent initiative.' Salas cut the connection.

Alvarez replaced the receiver, slumped back in the chair, put his feet up on the desk. He'd done his best and no man should reproach himself when he could say that.

He needed to question Ogden again, but time for reflection would not go amiss; he'd wait until the afternoon.

Alvarez parked in front of Ca'n Nou and crossed the gravel drive to the front door, rang the bell. The door was opened by Concha. 'What do you want now?' she said with curt hostility.

'To talk to the señor.'

'He's not here.'

'Have you any idea when he'll be back?'

'How can I tell? I'm preparing supper, but perhaps he will be too drunk to want to eat.'

'Is he still upset?'

'Sweet Mary, what kind of a person are you? His wife dies and you ask me if he is still upset!'

'It's not every bereaved husband who is.'

'You would bury a wife with a smile, not a tear? . . . Unlike you, he grieves until it hurts to watch. Why won't you leave him alone?'

'I need to ask him questions.'

'You have not asked enough to make yourself feel important?'

'I'm investigating the death of his wife . . .'

'Which anyone but a heartless fool would know had nothing to do with him ... I tell you this, any woman who married you would get even less than she expected!' She slammed the door shut.

She was probably right, he thought as he made his way back to the car. What did he have to offer? Only a belief in the ultimate triumph of justice. In the present age, such a belief tended to be a liability, not an asset.

He settled behind the wheel. Was there value in what he'd just heard? Concha was not someone to see true emotion because it was conventional wisdom that there should be emotion to be seen. She was convinced Ogden's grieving was genuine. But was he grieving because his wife had died, or because her death had not gone unquestioned as planned?

As Alvarez entered the house, he could hear Dolores singing a song which contained strange, disturbing notes that identified a Moorish origin. He carried on through to the dining-room and sat at the table opposite Jaime. He brought a glass out of the sideboard, helped himself to brandy, added three cubes of ice. He drank, then leaned forward and said in a low vocie: 'Have you given her a bunch of flowers or a box of chocolates?'

'Why would I go and do a thing like that?'

'How long has she been singing?'

'Ever since I got back from work. Yet only this morning she was snapping my head off.' He emptied his glass. 'If I live to be a thousand, I'll never understand women.'

'Does any man?'

'I had a cousin who used to boast he did, but when you met his wife you knew he was a liar.'

The singing stopped a moment before Dolores, red of face, sweating freely, pushed her way through the bead curtain. 'Good, you're back, Enrique. The meal would have been spoiled if you'd been late.'

'Is it something special, then?'

'I thought everyone would like pez espada o aguja palada.' She hurried back into the kitchen.

'It's a long time since she cooked that.' Alvarez drained his

153

glass, refilled it. 'Try and work out if it's something you've said or done that's put her into a good mood and then say or do it again.'

On Tuesday morning, it was once again Concha who opened the front door of Ca'n Nou. 'Haven't you anything better to do? Can't leave him alone, can you?' She glared at Alvarez before she reluctantly stepped to one side. 'He's out by the pool.'

He politely thanked her and received only a snort of dislike in return, made his way through to the patio. Ogden, his face grey and lined, wearing swimming trunks, was seated at the table on which was a bottle of gin, another of tonic, and an ice bucket. He looked up, but said nothing.

Alvarez sat. 'I should like to talk about the trip to the Peninsula I've just made. I first went to Son Jordi at the southern end of the Pyrenees.'

Ogden looked away, but not before Alvarez noticed his expression, which suggested he was shocked and desperately trying to pull his wits together. 'That's the nearest village to where your wife, Señora Belinda, supposedly suffered her accident. The mayor told me that the man she was with drove her straight into Las Macaulas because he knew there was no doctor in Son Jordi. D'you think he just guessed there wouldn't be, or did he know that?'

Ogden, with a shaking hand, poured himself another drink.

'The doctor pronounced her dead and called the undertaker. The undertaker got in touch with you regarding the funeral arrangements; after an initial refusal, you agreed to pay for a cremation. Apparently, all very straightforward. Only it seems she was walking in the mountains with her friend and she fell over a rock face. That exactly matches Señora Sabrina's accident. Wouldn't you call that a strange coincidence?'

'Why ask me?'

'Didn't you scout the area around Son Jordi very thoroughly to find somewhere where the accident could supposedly take place?'

'That's a filthy suggestion.'

'At Son Brau, you and your wife were received as guests. There, you indulged in the English pleasure of walking the estate. Of course, your wife had no idea that you were searching for somewhere suitable to stage a second, but this time genuine, "accident".'

'I never walked around that place. I can't walk as I used to.'

It was time for a lie. 'Señor Zafortega told me that you both had been guests more than once and you always asked if he minded if you went for a walk.'

'He's wrong. If anyone went, it was Sabrina on her own. I've just told you, I couldn't.'

'You both went. She thought it was to be another faked accident, you knew you were going to murder her.'

'No!' Ogden shouted, his face strained, his lips trembling.

Concha hurried out of the house. 'What's wrong?' she demanded breathlessly.

'Nothing,' Alvarez replied shortly.

'Then why is the señor shouting in pain?'

'The truth is often painful.'

'What do you know about truth? You, who ask if he is grieving.'

'I'm doing my job . . .'

'Then if you were even half a man, you would find another job.' She switched to Castilian and spoke very simply and slowly to Ogden. 'Your food is prepared, señor.' She briefly stared at Alvarez with contempt, turned on her heels and went back into the house.

Alvarez silently swore. The tension, born of guilt and fear, built up until Ogden had been on the point of confessing, had now been dissipated, thanks to Concha's intervention, and it would be very difficult, probably impossible, to regenerate it. Nevertheless, he doggedly continued the questioning. 'The next coincidence was the fact that the doctor who issued the certificate on Señora Belinda's death retired soon after he had done so, even though well short of retiring age. Clearly, he came into a large sum of money . . .'

'You think I killed Sabrina? Why would I kill someone who meant everything to me?' Ogden demanded wildly.

'For the two reasons that so often lead to murder – jealousy and money. Although you had swindled an insurance company out of a very large sum, your wife had extravagant tastes and you knew that you could not go on spending at the same rate, yet you could be certain that if you did not continue to indulge her, she would leave you for a man who could. The only solution to this problem was to commit a second insurance fraud. But having reached that conclusion, you suddenly learned that she was having an affair, jealousy drove you to decide that this time the insurance claim would be genuine because she would indeed be dead . . .'

'Short of money? I know where to invest because I've friends back in the City who'll give the nod on inside information if they're certain it can't ever be traced back and there's something in it for them. I'm richer now than when I left England.'

'Can you prove that?'

'How d'you think I could afford to buy the bracelet if I was short?'

'What bracelet?'

'The one she saw . . .' He stopped, swallowed heavily several times, began to blubber. Tears trickled down his cheeks and his mouth worked as if he were chewing something.

After a while, Alvarez asked a second time: 'What bracelet?'

He regained a measure of self-control and spoke in a flat voice, now devoid of any trace of hysteria. 'One of the diamonds in the emerald ring was loose. We took it to a jeweller's in Palma to have it reset and they'd a sapphire bracelet on view. She loved sapphires because of her mother . . .' He became silent.

'She saw this bracelet,' Alvarez prompted.

'She kept looking at it and the assistant egged her on, like they always do, and said how someone with real taste would buy it . . . I made out I didn't realize how much she liked it. But a few days later I bought it for her. I hoped . . .'

'What did you hope?'

'That she'd realize how much I could give her and so would never want to leave me.'

'When did you buy it?'

156

'Just before her birthday. She guessed what it was before she unwrapped the package, but wouldn't open up for a long time in case she was wrong. She looked . . . She looked . . .' He began to cry once more.

'What's the name of the jeweller's?'

'Joyeria Roldan,' he mumbled.

'Where's the bracelet now?'

'In the safe. When she took it out of its case, she told me she was the luckiest woman in the world . . . Lucky? When she's dead?' His voice suddenly rose. 'And you can think I killed her?'

Back in the office, Alvarez phoned Joyeria Roldan. He spoke to a superior woman who passed him on to an even more superior man.

'It is not our policy to discuss our clients' business with third parties.'

'The police have the powers to change policies,' Alvarez said shortly.

'What was the name?'

'Ogden.' He had to spell it out.

There was a pause, then: 'Señor Ogden purchased a sapphire bracelet on the twenty-third of June.'

'How much did it cost?'

'Four million five hundred thousand pesetas.'

'Has Señor Ogden recently asked you to repurchase it?'

'Of course not.' The tone made it clear that Joyeria Roldan took care not to do business with that kind of customer.

After ringing off, Alvarez settled back in the chair. Would a man spend four and a half million pesetas buying jewellery for his wife when he intended to kill her within days? Unlikely. Unless, of course, he was sufficiently sharp-witted to realize that to do so would be to underpin his apparent innocence. Could any amateur summon up the acting skills to simulate the raw grief which had seemingly overwhelmed Ogden?

Where lay the truth?

Some facts were certain. With the help of Belinda/Sabrina, Ogden had carried out an insurance fraud. In Mallorca, the two of them had led an extravagant life, but it seemed his

157

wealth could sustain that. But she had not learned that the gods never fulfilled all wishes, or humans might become gods and so instead of being content with what she had, she had yearned for more – the passion of youth.

Some facts seemed certain. Sabrina's death could have been accident or murder and motive would determine which. The motive? She had discovered Ruffolo was also having an affair with Carol and, maddened by jealousy, had threatened to betray him to Ada unless he threw Carol aside. But evidence said her affair with Ruffolo had ended amicably long before her death. Ogden, having planned to defraud a second insurance company, had learned of Sabrina's infidelity and determined to gain revenge as well as a further half million pounds. But he had bought her a very expensive bracelet which was hardly the act of a man intending to murder. And his grief seemed genuine.

Some facts were very uncertain. Keane was at an age when a man might seek the favours of a younger woman not simply for the physical pleasure, but also for the psychological reassurance to be gained from proving he could still attract. Initially, he had appeared to be reluctant to repeat the rumour concerning the liaison between Sabrina and Ruffolo, yet after very little persuasion he had done so. Had he initiated the rumour – and in truth was happy to spread it – because he had tried to have an affair with Sabrina, but had been rejected? His wife's behaviour could suggest she thought this possible, even while she struggled to deny the possibility. Yet such behaviour could simply signify no more than the attempt, which any loyal wife would make, to defend her husband from a baseless charge. Was he using his warped and hurtful humour to conceal the corroding bitterness which came from learning that he could no longer attract? Could such bitterness, however corroding, ever lead to murder? That seemed doubtful, even if there were times when motive bore little relation to the crime it spawned.

Some facts were mere conjectures. Sabrina had betrayed her husband once, so she had done so many times. When she and Ruffolo had ended their affair, she had sought another man to provide the passion that her husband could not. And because this new lover had had to conceal their affair as carefully as she, they had chosen to meet in the mountains behind Son Brau because there the odds of being discovered were virtually nil. Their passion, perversely heightened and sharpened because of its illicitness, had left them with little regard to the world beyond themselves. She had fallen over the rock face. Terrified by the consequences should he report the death, he had stripped her of all means of identification and made it appear she had left the island . . . Yet in a community where malicious gossip was a staple, it seemed there had been no whisper of yet another man in her life . . .

There surely was a logical conclusion to be drawn? Alvarez settled more comfortably in the chair, rested his feet on the desk and closed his eyes. Since there was no sustainable motive for murder, whatever the actual circumstances surrounding Sabrina's death, it had been an accident . . .

CHAPTER 23

On Wednesday, life was peaceful until Isabel returned home for lunch. She entered the dining-room in a rush that brought her hard up against one of the armchairs. 'Guess what?' She began to giggle.

Jaime refilled his glass. 'What are you going on about?'

'You've got to guess.'

'You've found the winning lottery ticket in the gutter?'

'Of course I haven't.'

'Inés has invited you to a party?'

'I wouldn't go if she did. You're not trying. Uncle, you guess.'

Alvarez said: 'Juan's in trouble.'

Her disappointment was immediate. 'Someone told you.'

'No.'

'They must have done.'

'Hand on heart, fingers straight, no one's said anything.'

'Then how do you know?'

Before he could explain that her satisfaction had been too obvious, Dolores came through the bead curtain. She looked beyond Isabel. 'Where's Juan?'

'Guess.'

'I'm too busy for ridiculosities. Nothing's happened to him, has it?' Her imagination began to move into overdrive.

'Something has.'

'Oh, my God! He's been hit by a car because he will run across the road even though I had told him time and again to walk. Is he badly hurt?' She swung round to face Jaime. 'Stop drinking yourself stupid and get ready to drive into Palma.'

'Hang on . . .'

'Can you not hurry yourself even for your own son who may be bleeding to death?'

160

'She hasn't said he's even been hurt.'

Dolores turned back. 'Has he?'

Frightened by the emotional furore she had raised, Isabel looked down at her shoes.

'Will you tell me,' cried Dolores, accepting her daughter's response as evidence that in some way or another, her worst fears were about to be justified. 'How seriously is he injured?'

'He isn't,' she mumbled.

Dolores's voice rose. 'You frighten me until my heart stops and then tell me he is unhurt? You are going to learn . . .' She stopped as they heard the front door slam shut.

Juan entered the dining-room to come to an abrupt stop as he found himself the centre of sharp interest. He nervously shifted his weight from one foot to the other.

'Well?' said Dolores, in her most magisterial tones.

Juan looked quickly at his sister, but she kept her gaze fixed firmly on her shoes.

'Have you had an accident?'

He shook his head.

'Are you in some sort of trouble?'

'Not really.'

'Either you are or you aren't.'

'It's beastly Old Long Nose. He never listens to me and just blows me up when it's not my fault . . .'

'What has happened?'

'Nothing.'

'Don't be stupid. If your teacher has been criticizing you then it is because you have misbehaved in rapaso.'

'It was . . .'

'Yes?'

'Her copying me.'

'You have again been guilty of copying?'

'I keep telling you, I didn't,' he cried, equal measures of fear and outrage at life's iniquities raising the pitch of his voice. 'It was Spanish grammar and I knew Blanca would copy from me so I deliberately made some mistakes. When Old Long Nose checked our books and saw the same mistakes, he said I'd copied her. But it wasn't me, it was her.'

'You admit that you intended deliberately to get Blanca into trouble?'

'That's what she did to me with arithmetic.'

'Two wrongs do not make a right.'

'But they make one feel a sight better,' murmured Jaime.

Dolores had very keen hearing. She whirled round. 'Small wonder our son behaves as he does when his father believes it right to seek satisfaction from another's misfortune!'

'Who's doing that? All I was saying was . . .'

'What you have to say is of very small account except when it encourages others into trouble.' She turned back. 'Juan, your lunch will be bread, oil, and tomato and you will eat it in your room so that you can think about your wickedness.'

'But I keep telling you, it wasn't me . . .'

'Go upstairs.'

He hesitated, then ran across to the stairs and up them.

She spoke to Isabel. 'And you also will eat lunch in your room.'

'Why me?'

'So that you can think how cruel you were to frighten your mother into an early grave.'

'I didn't. It was you who went on about him being hurt . . .'

'Go upstairs.'

She crossed to the stairs, eyes glinting with tears, and climbed them very slowly.

Dolores reached across the table to pick up the bottle of brandy. 'For once we will have a meal when you two have not drunk yourselves stupid.' She marched back into the kitchen.

'How did all that happen from nothing?' Jaime asked plaintively as he stared at his empty glass.

Alvarez adjusted the angle of the fan, wriggled his head into a more comfortable position on the pillow and sighed with pleasure. The gods had been generous when they had given man the siesta.

Infuriatingly, for once sleep eluded him. He heard the distant church clock strike the half hour. Age was said to make sleep increasingly difficult, but surely he was not yet that old? Perhaps he was ill? Panicking, he mentally examined himself from head to toe, but he could find no stabbing pain, no dull agony, that was the harbinger of impending death.

The church clock struck the hour. He swore, with all the crudity that the Mallorquin language so generously offered. Was he from now on to be denied all rest, like some land-locked Flying Dutchman?

Sleep had finally almost claimed him when into his mind slid the memory of Juan's expression of outrage at the injustice of being punished because his planned revenge on Blanca had backfired. In later years, perhaps he would have cause to be grateful that he had been young when he'd learned that the female was indeed more deadly than the male . . .

Suddenly, he was once more wide awake. In truth, any plan could backfire, more especially when it was fuelled by greed and conceived by a female.

CHAPTER 24

When Alvarez entered the kitchen, Dolores, her face expressing sharp surprise, looked up at the electric clock on the wall. 'It's not yet five. I've not made the coffee.'

'That's all right. I don't want anything.'

'Are you ill?'

'Just in a hurry.'

Concern gave way to suspicion. 'Why?'

'I have to question someone.'

'A woman, no doubt?'

'As a matter of fact, yes.'

'A foreigner?'

'English.'

'And so much younger than you that it shreds a respectable woman's heart even to think about it. Aiyee! When a man is born a fool, even the Good Lord cannot restrain his stupidities.'

'She's very considerably older than me and long since gone to seed. She's also very, very rich.'

Dolores fidgeted with a plastic bowl that was on the table; eventually, she said, her tone now reflective: 'When the woman is older, she has had more experience of the ridiculous ways of men. And there comes a time when a man, if he has any intelligence at all, realizes that comfortable security is far more important than a beautiful face.'

'You think she'd make me a good wife?'

'There must be some foreign women who lead decent lives.'

'Sadly, she hardly qualifies on that count. Her present indulgence is an Italian lad a third her age.'

She said, with sudden fury: 'So it amuses you to make fun of me?'

'It rankles to have you assuming I have only to speak to a foreign woman to start lusting after her.'

'What else, when experience tells me that that is so?'

He did not pursue the point since she had a good memory.

As he drove to Parelona, he caught the first glimpse of the hotel, the small bay, and the mountains which backed it. There, was great beauty; there, was great ugliness. Did the one always have to shadow the other because life needed both?

He parked behind a green Alfa Romeo in front of Ca Na Ada and climbed out of his car to hear the sounds of splashing water. Beauty came in many guises. He walked towards the front door, came to a stop as he changed his mind, turned to go round the side of the house to the pool. If in luck, he would find Ruffolo on his own. He proved to be in luck.

As Ruffolo looked up from the patio mattress, the sun glinted on his reflective sunglasses; he turned over on to his back and propped himself up on his elbows. 'The British say a bad penny keeps turning up,' he said sneeringly.

'And we say, a dead sheep attracts many flies.' Alvarez came to a halt a metre from the mattress. 'There are some more questions I need to ask you.'

'I've told you everything I can.'

'It is what you have not said that now interests me.'

Even though the glasses masked Ruffolo's eyes, it was obvious that the Delphic quality of the comment worried him.

'It is too hot in the sun, so shall we move into the shade?'

'I'm staying here.'

'Then I will have to shout my questions and you will have to shout your answers. I think that will be tiring for both of us.' Alvarez crossed to the shade of the pool complex and sat.

After a while, Ruffolo, assuming an attitude of amused resignation, joined Alvarez. 'Let's get it over quickly,' he said, as he sat.

'When Señora Sabrina Ogden saw you with Señorita Carol Murdoch, she was very upset, was she not?'

'I've been though all that before.'

'And now we'll go through it again.'

'Like hell. I know nothing about Sabrina's death. Ada's

told you enough times for even you to understand, she and me were together all that Sunday and Monday.'

'Surely the señorita usually enjoys a siesta?'

'She's explained she didn't have one either afternoon.'

'Perhaps she said that because you managed to persuade her you had nothing to do with Señora Ogden's disappearance and therefore it would save a lot of annoyance if she told me the little lie?'

'You can't give one reason for me killing Sabrina.'

'On the contrary, I can suggest two. First, to prevent her telling Señorita Heron about her affair with you.'

'Sabrina and me had finished. Hans confirmed I hadn't taken her to his pad in months.'

'There are many other places for an assignation.'

'Can you prove we were still together?'

'No.'

'Of course you can't, since we weren't. So forget it.'

'Secondly,' said Alvarez equably, 'to prevent anyone realizing that you were an accomplice to the intended murder of her husband.'

'Are you completely crazy?' Ruffolo shouted.

'You hold a fatal attraction for women – why, is a complete mystery – and when Señora Ogden discovered you were having an affair with another woman, she was desperate to find a way of regaining your sole affection. That you were content to live with Señorita Heron in the circumstances in which you did, showed you would do anything to enjoy a life of idle luxury. This convinced her – although to an onlooker it would seem that your affair with her would suggest otherwise – that if she had enough money, you would be hers and hers alone.

'When she married, her husband had been a wealthy man. But then he suffered financial problems so severe that he decided to carry out, with her help, an insurance fraud. It was cleverly planned and executed and the company concerned had to accept the claim as genuine and they paid him half a million pounds. This enabled him to recover financially and even, after a short while, to become wealthier than before.

'When someone experiences a disaster but recovers, if he

has any sense he takes great care to try not to suffer a similar disaster again. That was why Señor Ogden, determined they should lead a less profligate life, took every opportunity to persuade her that they had to be much more careful with money – probably even to the extent of saying they were having to spend capital. This convinced her that if things went on as they were – and in her mind, luxurious presents did not logically contradict what he'd told her, they merely confirmed that he was totally besotted with her and would suffer ruin again rather than lose her – it would not be long before all his money was gone and then she'd have lost you for all time. It was this conviction which led her to decide her husband must die.

'She could be certain you'd never worry how she came into money, so she told you why she'd soon be a wealthy widow. You persuaded her that if it ever became known you and she had had an affair, it must appear that it had long since come to an end in order to prevent any suspicion that she could have a motive for her husband's death.

'She believed she had found the perfect way of killing her husband. He was much older than she and inevitably not as virile as he would wish: she made him very aware of his inadequacies. It then became easy to persuade him to seek relief in a supposed aphrodisiac – which also happened to be a poison. He was very careful about the amount of cantharides he took, but she found the opportunity to feed him what she hoped was a fatal dose, believing that if the cause of death was established, it would be accepted with many a snigger that he had tried to become too much of a man.

'He nearly died, but not quite. Suffering the fears that failure raised, she turned to you for the reassurance she so desperately needed. She demanded you leave the señorita and she'd leave her husband and together you'd find happiness. It was not a future to attract you. Give up the luxury and embrace poverty in the name of love? You told her to stay with her husband, hoping the truth would remain hidden, and to call you when he died from natural causes. Shocked by your cynical coldness and made ever more desperate by it, she replied that if you didn't do as she demanded, she'd tell Señorita Heron the truth about your relationships with her and Señorita Murdoch, which must result in your being thrown out of this house.

'It seemed you were doomed to a future of hardship whichever alternative you accepted. But you were as determined to continue to enjoy life here as she was to hold on to you. How to silence her? No doubt you promised her your undying love if only she'd wait, but she had gained a more realistic idea of what your promises were worth and so demanded results, not words. It became clear that your only way of escape would be to kill her.

'She had told you all about the insurance swindle and so you could employ many of the details in your plans for her murder. You knew she and her husband had been several times to Son Brau and that much of the estate was wooded mountainside of no commercial value and rarely, if ever, visited. You went there often, while Señorita Heron had an alcoholic siesta, and eventually found the exact site you wanted. This meant that there was every chance the body would remain undiscovered until it couldn't be identified since you would strip off every means of identification and lay a trail which would make it seem Señora Ogden had returned to England within a day of disappearing. But you were smart enough to recognize that things don't always go according to plan, so you would make certain it would be virtually impossible to tell whether the fall had been an accident or murder. And by choosing a method of murder that exactly matched the faked accident Señora Belinda was supposed to have suffered, if murder were ever suspected, Señor Ogden must be the prime suspect.'

Ruffolo stood and crossed to the refrigerator, brought out a tray of ice and a bottle of tonic, picked up the bottle of gin on the nearby table, poured himself a drink. He returned to his chair. 'Can you prove she was pushed over the cliff and didn't just trip?'

'Motive makes murder by far the more likely.'

'What motive? She and me made waves? That was finished and you've admitted you can't prove otherwise. Who's seen us together in the past months? Did I ever get in touch with her on the mobile? Can you even prove that the old fool didn't take an overdose because he thought it would be more effective?'

'No, I can't.'

'Ada says I was here that Sunday and Monday which makes all your ideas just crap. Clear off and leave me in peace.'

'It's interesting that not once have you expressed any affection for the señora or regrets at her death. A man's attitude sometimes tells much more than he wishes to be told. Yours tells me I am right.'

'I must have murdered her because I'm not weeping? It's no wonder the law on this island is a joke.'

A door banged and they both looked in the direction of the house to see Ada walk slowly towards them. She wore a brightly coloured, voluminous garment that billowed with every step, making her body appear gross rather than merely fat; the harsh sunlight picked out the blotchy, sagging flesh of her face and in a final act of cruelty, the hairs above her mouth.

Wheezing, she slumped down on a chair. 'Gawd, I've a head!'

Ruffolo stood and crossed to stand behind her. He stroked her forehead with his fingertips. 'My poor angel. Let me get you your pills.'

'I took two and they're bloody useless.'

'The doctor said you could have up to four.'

'If I have that many, they give me frightful bellyache.'

'Why is it that the wonderful people always suffer the worst?'

A whisper of breeze brought them the sounds of children playing on the beach; a chorus of cicadas suddenly started shrilling, as if to a conductor's baton.

'What's he want?' she demanded, jerking a thumb in the direction of Alvarez.

'Would you like a good laugh?'

'Not with my bloody head!'

'He's accusing me of having murdered Sabrina! It doesn't matter you've told him endless times that I was with you, that he has to admit he can't be certain she didn't fall accidentally, that he's not a whisper of proof that I worked with Sabrina to murder the old fool of a husband of hers . . .'

'You what?' she said violently, then grimaced with pain.

Ruffolo quickened the rate at which he stroked her forehead. 'Could anything be more absurd? Obviously, he's so incompetent that the job's overwhelmed him.'

'Clear off my property,' she said to Alvarez, her voice harsh and ugly.

'Señorita, do you still claim the señor was with you throughout the Sunday afternoon on which Señora Ogden disappeared and on the following Monday?'

'Of course I do.'

'I am sure you are lying.'

'Prove it,' jeered Ruffolo.

'Perhaps I can.'

'You reckon to do the impossible?'

'We have a saying, Even the impossible may become possible if one has sufficient imagination or a rich uncle.'

Ruffolo spoke to Ada. 'My angel, we'll have to telephone someone in authority and say we're being bothered by an inspector who's mentally ill.'

Ada stared at Alvarez. 'So what's your line – imagination or a rich uncle?'

'Don't encourage him, my sweet . . .' Ruffolo began.

'Well, which is it?' Her harshly spoken words cut across his softly spoken ones.

Alvarez answered her. 'Señorita, the character of a suspect can become a very important arrow.'

'What's that supposed to mean?'

'It can point to probability.'

'You're still talking in riddles.'

'The señor is a man for whom right and wrong are merely the difference between what he does, and what he does not, want. His standards are formed by greed.'

'Surely you're not going to let him insult me like that?' Ruffolo said aggressively.

She ignored him.

'When someone has suffered great poverty and then enjoyed the pleasures of plenty,' Alvarez continued, 'his greed can become so all-consuming it even overwhelms his natural cunning.'

'I still don't understand,' she said.

'When a man commits a crime and keeps the evidence of his guilt, he must either be a fool or consumed with greed. The señor is certainly no fool.'

'What evidence?'

'When Señora Ogden died, she was stripped of everything that could identify her; included was her sapphire-and-diamond engagement ring, valued at twelve thousand pounds. To someone who has always lived by his wits, it must have been obvious that the ring was valuable; to someone consumed by greed, it would have been impossible to throw the ring away. He will keep it until he can travel to Naples where he knows all the best markets for stolen goods.'

She turned to look at Ruffolo, said fiercely: 'You've been trying to get me to go to Naples.'

'My love, you kept saying how tired you felt and I decided you needed a change and it would be fun to visit Italy; I never mentioned Naples.'

'You told me we'd go there to celebrate our first meeting.'

'I said we'd celebrate, wherever we were. Because I mentioned our first meeting, you automatically thought of Naples.'

She was trying to remember more clearly because she could not immediately still her doubts, Alvarez thought. How to increase them to the point where they finally forced her to tell the truth? The answer was obvious, but he hesitated before he spoke to Ruffolo because his words could only cause her pain. 'Señorita Carol will confirm that you told her you were going to Naples for a holiday.' He managed to speak with conviction.

'I've never told her any –' Ruffolo came to a sudden stop.

'Who's Carol?' Ada demanded.

'A friend,' Alvarez answered. 'A very close friend of his.'

'I don't know anyone of that name,' Ruffolo protested roughly.

'She'll be most upset to hear that.' The bolder the lie, the more likely it was to be believed. 'After all, she told me that you've assured her you intend to leave Señorita Heron to be with her.'

Ada made a sound that was not quite a cry.

'My very precious,' Ruffolo said urgently, 'don't listen to him. He's trying to trick you.'

'Who's Carol?' she asked a second time.

'I've told you, I don't know anyone of that name.'

'Perhaps, señorita,' Alvarez said, 'it will be best if I bring Señorita Carol here so you can judge for yourself what is the truth.'

'No!' Ruffolo shouted.

'Why not?'

He tried to speak with greater composure. 'You'll just teach her to lie.'

'Then let us all drive to the port now and talk to her before I have a chance to say anything. And afterwards we might speak to Señor Wilms who lives in the flat where she and you made love whenever you could escape from here, unnoticed because the señorita was enjoying a siesta, prolonged by your help.'

'Another goddamn lie!'

'No doubt Carlos, Marta, and Inés, will be able to confirm or deny that you often have driven away in the afternoons.'

Ruffolo began to stroke Ada's neck with his fingers. 'Ada, my only love, we've suffered enough of this stupidity . . .'

'Tell the staff to come here.'

'But . . .'

'Now!'

'Can't you see that asking them will make me look – '

She interrupted him, her voice harsh. 'You're too bloody scared to do it!' She swung round to face Alvarez. 'I had a very long siesta on that Sunday and Monday because he made me drink too much. I've no idea where he was.'

Ruffolo spoke pleadingly. 'How can you be so cruel to someone who loves you more than life itself?'

Alvarez said: 'Where is the engagement ring Señora Ogden was wearing when she died?'

'How could I know that, for God's sake?'

172

'Then you can have no objection to my searching your possessions.'

'I'm not letting some peasant rummage through my things.'

'I regret that you cannot prevent me since I have a search warrant.'

Ruffolo's expression tightened and for a couple of seconds he remained motionless. Then he dropped his hands away from Ada's neck, swung round, and raced towards the house.

Alvarez struggled to his feet and followed as quickly as he could; by the time he reached the outside door, he was short of breath and sweat was trickling down his face and back. Halfway across the sitting-room, he heard a door slam. Marta was in the hall. 'Where's he gone?' he panted.

She pointed at the doorway on her left.

Beyond this was a short passage which gave access to two rooms: the first, a bathroom, the door of the second proved to be locked. In his impotent anger, Alvarez shook the handle. 'You can't get away,' he shouted, in between gulping down air into his straining lungs.

He heard a car's engine start and rev fiercely; then the sound died away. He used a handkerchief to wipe the sweat from his face. Salas would call him a fool for not having realized Ruffolo would leave the bedroom through the window, race round to the Alfa Romeo, and drive off. But when things happened so quickly, it took a man time to catch up with events . . .

He slowly returned to the hall to find Marta was still there. 'What's the number of the car?'

She merely stared at him.

'The registration number of the Alfa Romeo – what is it?'

She shrugged her shoulders. 'How would I know?'

He used the phone to call Traffic. As he waited for the connection to be made, he wondered if panic would make Ruffolo forget that there was only the one road from Parelona to Port Llueso? When Traffic answered, he asked for an immediate roadblock to be set up just outside the port and to stop a green Alfa Romeo, and if the driver was Rino Ruffolo, to search him and the car for a sapphire-and-diamond ring. No, he did not

173

know the registration number of the car. Yes, he did realize there were many Alfas on the road . . . He cut the connection, dialled Guardia Operations in Palma and asked them to issue a stop order on Rino Ruffolo effective at all ports and airports. As he replaced the receiver, he despondently accepted that if Ruffolo reached the port before the roadblock could be set up, he'd probably overcome his panic sufficiently to realize that by far his best bet was not to try to escape the island immediately, but to lie low for several weeks. No watch remained sharp for very long.

'What's up?' Marta asked. 'Done something, has he? Pinched one of the señorita's rings?'

'Nothing belonging to her.'

'Oh!' She was disappointed. 'But it doesn't sound like he'll be coming back in a hurry.'

'I very much doubt he'll do that.'

'My horoscope said it would be a good day.'

He returned to the pool patio. Ada, looking far less care-worn, was silent until he sat, then said, her voice high: 'Well? Did you find a ring?'

'He locked the bedroom door, left through the window, and drove off.'

'So he's made a bloody fool of you?'

'That's easily done.'

'And you don't know if he did have the ring?'

'Would he have run if he hadn't?'

Alvarez sat and stared at the pool and watched the reflected sunlight shimmer as the water moved to the slightest of breezes.

'Was he screwing Sabrina?' she asked suddenly.

'Yes.'

'And Carol?'

'Yes.'

'Any more?'

'I don't know of any.'

There was a long silence which ended when Marta came out from the house and across to where they sat, a cordless phone in her hand. 'It's for you,' she said to Alvarez in Mallorquin.

'Who is it?' Ada asked in English.

'Probably one of my colleagues,' Alvarez said. As Marta returned to the house, he answered the call, which was brief. At the conclusion, he switched off the phone, placed it on the table. 'They stopped the car and searched him; he had a sapphire-and-diamond ring. It will have to be identified, of course, but there's no doubt it was Sabrina's.' He heard a throaty sound and turned to look at Ada. Her face was contorted and tears were rolling down her cheeks. Remorse gripped him. However futile the attempt must be, he tried to find words that would ease her agony. 'Señorita, he will have a fair trial. And there is now no death penalty in Spain so that . . .'

She said fiercely: 'They'll laugh at me; they'll jeer at me; they'll do everything to humiliate me.'

He realized he had completely misjudged the cause of her distress. She was concerned only with herself. Such monumental selfishness was ugly. Yet to offset this ugliness, she had in the past shown the courage to face hostility and not to succumb to hypocrisy.

She wiped her cheeks with her hand. 'I'll sell up and move.'

He tried to help her regain that courage. 'You'll meekly let them drive you away?'

'You think I can stay here with everyone knowing he was making a complete fool of me by screwing half the population when I wasn't looking?'

'Meet them head on, as you've always done. They'll expect you to feel humiliated, so laugh at what's happened; tell them it's fine by you because you were becoming very bored with him and this has saved the expense of getting rid of him; give the most extravagant party in honour of your new-found freedom. Leave them bewildered and more envious than ever.'

She went to speak, checked the words. She fiddled with the top button of the dress that so ill-suited her. 'I suppose, after all that, you want a drink?'

'I'll not refuse one.'

'For my money, you wouldn't bloody well know how to.

175

There's champagne in the refrigerator and probably some gin somewhere. If you want brandy, use the cordless to tell 'em in the house to bring some.'

He identified which button on the phone to press and when the call was answered, asked Marta for a bottle of Hors d'Age. There were times when a man did not dishonour himself by asking for the best.